W9-CSK-715

ABBY AND THE
BEST KID EVER

**Other books by
Ann M. Martin**

Leo the Magnificat
Rachel Parker, Kindergarten Show-off
Eleven Kids, One Summer
Ma and Pa Dracula
Yours Turly, Shirley
Ten Kids, No Pets
Slam Book
Just a Summer Romance
Missing Since Monday
With You and Without You
Me and Katie (the Pest)
Stage Fright
Inside Out
Bummer Summer

ABBY AND THE BEST KID EVER

Ann M. Martin

AN
APPLE
PAPERBACK

SCHOLASTIC INC.
New York Toronto London Auckland Sydney

The author gratefully acknowledges
Nola Thacker
for her help in
preparing this manuscript.

Cover art by Hodges Soileau

If you purchased this book without a cover, you should be aware that this book is stolen property. It was reported as "unsold and destroyed" to the publisher, and neither the author nor the publisher has received any payment for this "stripped book."

No part of this publication may be reproduced in whole or in part, or stored in a retrieval system, or transmitted in any form or by any means, electronic, mechanical, photocopying, recording, or otherwise, without written permission of the publisher. For information regarding permission, write to Scholastic Inc., Attention: Permissions Department, 555 Broadway, New York, NY 10012.

ISBN 0-590-05994-7

Copyright © 1998 by Ann M. Martin. All rights reserved. Published by Scholastic Inc. THE BABY-SITTERS CLUB, APPLE PAPERBACKS and logos are trademarks and/or registered trademarks of Scholastic Inc.

12 11 10 9 8 7 6 5 4 3 2 1   8 9/9 0 1 2 3/0

Printed in the U.S.A.   40

First Scholastic printing, February 1998

CHAPTER 1

What is short and full of holidays?

Summer?

Wrong.

The answer is winter. I mean, think about it: Christmas, Kwanzaa, Hanukkah, Martin Luther King Jr. Day, Valentine's Day, Presidents' Day, and I can't remember what else. Plus, February (the shortest, coldest month of the year) not only has *two* holidays, but it is Black History Month.

Holidays are good but why are most of them in the months when it is practically impossible to field a decent soccer team or enjoy a good run? (And where is a day for the women? Why don't we have Susan B. Anthony Day? Or Sojourner Truth Day? Puh-lease!)

I was brooding about this on the first Monday afternoon in February, to the mournful sound of violin scales. I was looking out to the gray, ice-encrusted sidewalk when the doorbell rang. I answered it and Kristy Thomas burst into my house like a breath of, well, practically spring air.

No, make that a hurricane.

But before I tell you about Kristy, I should tell you a little about myself. I'm Abby. Abigail Stevenson, formerly of Long Island, now of Stoneybrook, Connecticut. My mother, my twin sister, Anna, and I moved here recently when Mom got a big promotion and wanted to make a new start in a safe neighborhood after the death of my father. He died four years ago in a car wreck.

I didn't want to move. I felt as if we were leaving my father forever, somehow. But moving brought us closer together as a family and encouraged us to talk a little about what losing Dad meant. So the change of locale turned out to be okay.

Here, as on Long Island, I'm a soccer star, in pursuit of the Athlete of the Year title. I'm okay in school, have major allergies (cat litter, milk, shellfish — you name it), and have asthma. I'm hoping to outgrow both when I get older (it does happen), but meanwhile I have to be careful about what I eat, watch the pollen count in the spring, and carry a prescription inhaler (a sort of tube of asthma medicine from which you inhale) at all times.

My eight-minutes-older twin, Anna, is not athletic, asthmatic, or allergic (although she does have scoliosis). She plays the violin in the school orchestra and practices her music a couple of hours each day before dinner. In fact, music is one of the reasons Anna declined to join the Baby-sitters Club (or BSC) when membership was offered to both of us. However, she and Shannon, another BSC member, have become good friends.

Anna and I look alike, but we have different styles. We both have pointed faces, deep brown eyes, and dark curly hair. Also, we both wear contact lenses or glasses. But Anna's hair is shorter than mine (which is shoulder length) and she has bangs, while I don't.

Kristy is my neighbor, schoolmate, and fellow Baby-sitters Club member. Actually, she's the president of the BSC (more about that later) and one of the most outspoken, forceful people on the planet. She is also as stubborn as a *rock*. These are all qualities I usually admire, especially since I have them myself.

But I don't *always* admire them in Kristy. So after she burst in, I braced myself and said, "What is it? And don't tell me it's a fire, because it's too cold. A fire would freeze to death in this weather."

Kristy didn't laugh. Although she shares

many of my best qualities, my keen sense of humor is not one of them. She doesn't always laugh at my jokes.

"They're leaving," Kristy said.

"Who? The sexists? The racists? The politicians?" I asked.

"The Addisons!" she exclaimed, giving me a Look.

"The Addisons?" I repeated stupidly.

"Sean and Corrie," she said. "And their parents too, of course."

"Whoa. Why?"

"Mrs. Addison got a major job offer in Seattle." Kristy paused and added, "Washington."

"I know where Seattle is," I said. "It's all the way across the country. Wow, this is going to make baby-sitting for them *extremely* time-consuming. I mean, think about the commute."

Kristy gave me another Look and I decided to lay off the jokes. I just said, "I'll miss them."

This was no joke. Sean Addison is ten and Corrie is nine, and two siblings couldn't be more different. Corrie is friendly and outgoing and artistically talented. She is an easy baby-sitting charge and a naturally cool kid. Sean is musically talented. (At least I think he is. I couldn't carry a tune in a bucket, so I don't know for sure.) He plays the tuba. He is also moody and intense and takes things very personally. His over-the-top reactions have gotten him into trouble in the past and haven't made him easy to take care of, especially since he is not particularly fond of baby-sitters.

"I'll miss them too," Kristy agreed. "For a while there, I thought Sean was going to be in contention for the title of Worst Kid Ever, but he looks like he's starting to deal with his problems."

(Do you know what I think? I think Kristy has a soft spot for "bad" kids. She even grew to like Lou McNally, a previous recipient of the Worst Kid Ever title.)

"Corrie's nice too," Kristy added, and I hid a grin.

"Corrie's always been a nice kid," I agreed. "I bet Sean grows up to be a pretty nice person."

But we both knew that we probably wouldn't get to see what kind of person Sean grew up to be. Would he be wild and crazy? A mad scientist? A tuba wonder? A horror novelist?

We sighed.

Then Kristy said, to change the subject, "What have you been doing all afternoon?"

"Waiting for spring," I answered.

"Huh?"

"So I can play soccer. Run. Do *something*."

"How about homework?" Kristy asked slyly.

We'd reached my room by then. It was clear

by the way my books were neatly stacked on my desk that I hadn't even thought about doing homework yet.

"Thanks," I muttered. It was my turn to give Kristy a Look.

Kristy relented. "I haven't finished today's homework either. David Michael and I went to the Stoneybrook Community Center to pick up more material on the Black History Month exhibition. He's really excited about it and he wanted to take the information to class tomorrow when they talk about project ideas. That's where I ran into Mrs. Addison and heard the news."

"You are a natural news magnet," I observed. That's another thing I admire about Kristy. Not much happens without her finding out about it, especially when it has any impact on the BSC, which this news definitely did.

"Are you going to do a project?" I asked, switching the subject back to the exhibition.

All of the schools in Stoneybrook submit projects to the exhibition for Black History Month. The elementary-school students participate in class projects. At Stoneybrook Middle School, which I attend, participation is voluntary. If you volunteer, you get extra credit in history.

"I'm not sure yet," Kristy replied. "Maybe

not. I've got a lot going on right now and I'm not sure I can fit the work in. You?"

"I think I will," I said. "We didn't get to do things like this at my old school on Long Island. I think it might be fun." (Plus, there was the not-so-small matter of extra credit. I needed it, which was something I wasn't going to tell Kristy, naturally.)

"What are you going to do?" Kristy asked.

"I haven't decided yet," I said, as if I had a hundred possibilities in mind. (Ha!)

Kristy looked at her watch. "Omigosh, it's almost time! Why didn't you tell me?"

I didn't have to ask "Time for what?" I knew. It was almost time for our Monday afternoon meeting of the BSC. We meet every Monday, Wednesday, and Friday afternoon at five-thirty sharp at Claudia Kishi's house, which is across town. And Kristy is never, ever late.

She grabbed my arm. "Let's go!"

"A coat!" I cried. "I need a coat. And gloves and . . ."

But Kristy was already bundling me out of the house. I had to snatch a coat off the back door rack and put it on as Kristy dragged me to her house. Her brother Charlie, who gives us a ride to the meetings, was just walking to his car when we reached her house.

"Hurry," Kristy cried.

Charlie knew better than to argue. He hurried. We reached Claudia's house with three minutes to spare.

Did I say I couldn't run in the winter in Stoneybrook? Wrong. Kristy and I ran up the front walk, ran through the front door, and ran up the stairs to Claudia's room. In one motion, Kristy stripped off her coat and threw herself into the director's chair, where she always sits.

"This meeting of the Baby-sitters Club will now come to order," she announced. "And wait until you hear the news. . . ."

CHAPTER 2

This was not the first time Kristy had opened a meeting with a dramatic announcement. You know what? It works every time. The entire group, all six of us, looked at her. Even *I* looked at her, and I already knew what the news was.

"The Addisons are moving," Kristy burst out, and Claudia, who had just stood up to take a book off her bookshelf to search for a missing half-eaten bag of M&Ms, sat down with a shocked look on her face.

(I remembered then that Claudia is probably the closest of the BSC members to the Addisons, since she and Corrie share an interest in art.)

The questions flew thick and fast, except from Claudia, who sat there, her head turning back and forth as if she were watching a play. When we quieted down, Stacey McGill, the BSC's treasurer and Claudia's best friend, said, "Claudia? Are you okay?"

Claudia looked at the book she was holding in one hand and the bag of candy in the other. She put the book down and took out a handful of M&Ms. She separated out the green ones and ate them. Then she said, "Well, Seattle has a very good reputation, artistically speaking."

We all laughed at that, and Claudia smiled. It was a true Claudia moment. No, it was a true BSC moment.

So maybe it's time I filled you in on BSC facts and BSC members.

We have seven full-time members: Kristy, our president; Claudia, vice-president; Mary Anne Spier, secretary; Stacey, treasurer; me, alternate officer; and Jessica Ramsey and Mallory Pike, junior officers. Jessi and Mal are junior officers because they are in sixth grade (the rest of us are eighth-graders) and can't accept babysitting jobs at night (except for their families). Our two associate members, Shannon Kilbourne and Logan Bruno, fill in as needed and don't have to attend meetings all the time (meetings are mandatory for full-time members). We also have one honorary member, Dawn Schafer, who used to be the alternate officer before she moved to California.

We meet at Claudia's because she has her own phone line, which means we don't tie up the Kishi family phone while we take job calls.

Clients know they can call during meeting

hours and reach not one but up to nine reliable baby-sitters. We hand over club dues to Stacey every Monday (and always groan about it). The dues help pay Claudia's phone bills, gas money for Charlie, plus necessary things such as pizza and snacks (Claudia always has a generous supply of snack food hidden around her room) and items for our Kid-Kits.

Kid-Kits are boxes (each of us has one) that we have decorated, filled with puzzles, games, books, stickers, and art materials. Some of the things in the kits are recycled, such as old toys and puzzles that BSC siblings have outgrown, and others are new. The Kid-Kits are our secret weapon in the BSC war against bored and restless kids. We don't take them on every job, but we use them strategically — when meeting new clients, when baby-sitting for a child who has been sick in bed, or when confronting a group of stir-crazy charges who've been inside too long because of snow or rain.

We keep three notebooks: the club record book, the club notebook, and the club mystery notebook.

The club record book, which contains the names, addresses, phone numbers, and other pertinent information about each of our clients, is Mary Anne's responsibility. She has never, ever made a mistake. The record book also contains each of our individual schedules and the

11

details about any baby-sitting job we accept.

The club notebook is a diary in which each member writes up every job she goes on, and we are all responsible for keeping up to speed on one another's entries. That way we stay up to date about what is happening in our clients' lives (for example, who is teething or learning to ride a bicycle). We can use the experiences from past jobs to deal with similar situations.

The mystery notebook is our most recent addition, started because we keep getting involved in mysteries. We use it to keep track of lists of clues, suspects, and strange occurrences. Mal is unofficially in charge of it.

As you can see, we are very organized. That's because we have some *formidably* organized people in the BSC, beginning with Madame President, Kristy.

In fact, the BSC was her idea. It came to her one night as she listened to her mother make one phone call after another in search of a baby-sitter for Kristy's younger brother, David Michael. Suddenly, Kristy thought that it would be great if a person could make just one phone call and reach several baby-sitters at once.

Kristy came up with the idea on a Tuesday afternoon. Practically the next day, she had put her idea into action, recruiting her best friend, Mary Anne (who lived next door), Claudia

12

(who lived across the street), and Claudia's friend Stacey. Soon Dawn, who had recently arrived in town, followed, then Logan and Shannon. Mal and Jessi joined soon after. Then when Dawn moved to California and it became clear that more baby-sitters were needed to handle all the work, I was recruited.

Kristy is possibly the world's most organized human being. Not only is she president of the BSC but she also coaches the Krushers (a little-kids' softball team), does well in school, and has played on the SMS softball team. According to Mary Anne, who's known Kristy since they were babies, Kristy has been like this all her life.

This might be because Kristy is from a big family and took on a lot of responsibility early in her life. You see, her father left the family when Kristy was pretty young, leaving Mrs. Thomas (who had a job in Stamford) with David Michael, Kristy, and her two older brothers, Charlie and Sam.

Then one day Kristy's mother met Watson Brewer, the CEO (Chief Executive Officer) of Unity Insurance, and they fell in love and got married. Kristy and her family moved across town from an ordinary (and sort of crowded) house on Bradford Court to a mansion with three floors and nine bedrooms. Her family also got *much* bigger and now includes Watson; Karen and Andrew, his two children from his first marriage; Emily Michelle, a new younger sister from Vietnam who was adopted by Kristy's mom and Watson; Kristy's grandmother, Nannie, who moved in to help out with Emily; plus a cranky cat, a large puppy, assorted goldfish, and possibly a ghost (at least, that's what Karen Brewer, who is seven, believes).

Kristy is the shortest person in our entire class. This means she naturally speaks up extra loudly to make sure she is heard. Some people call her bossy, as if that were a bad thing, but it isn't, except when she tries to boss me.

Kristy shares my love of sports, although she's not the full-time jock I am. She's also a dog person (in fact, she wears a cap with a collie on it, in memory of her collie, Louie, who died). And if that cap isn't a tip-off, I should add that Kristy is not terribly concerned with fashion. She has brown eyes and long brown hair, never uses makeup, and wears a variation of the same outfit almost every day: jeans, sweater or sweatshirt, and sneakers. We call this her uniform.

Mary Anne is not a sports fan, does not come from a large family, and is shy and caring. Even though she is also short and can be as stubborn as Kristy, I do not always understand how they can be best friends. But they are.

14

Mary Anne was raised as an only child. Her mother died when Mary Anne was just a baby and her father raised her by himself. He was loving but very strict and protective. Mary Anne has had to work hard to convince him that she's grown-up enough to take some responsibility herself — that she can choose her own clothes (she switched from little-kid outfits to a sort of casual preppy style) and *not* wear her brown hair in the two pigtails she'd had since she was small.

Mary Anne is very sensitive (even sad commercials can make her cry). She is also a good listener and was the first of the BSC members to have a steady boyfriend (fellow BSC member Logan, about whom you will hear more later). She also has a kitten named Tigger.

If you wonder how Mary Anne could persuade her father that she was grown-up enough to have a kitten — *and* a boyfriend — you should know that Mr. Spier has loosened up since he got married to his former high school sweetheart, who also happens to be Dawn Schafer's mother.

Mrs. Schafer, Dawn, and Dawn's younger brother, Jeff, moved back to Stoneybrook from California after the Schafers' divorce, and Dawn and Mary Anne became best friends and fellow BSC members. Then they discovered that Mrs. Schafer and Mr. Spier had had a high school romance and they went to work to help rekindle it. Before you could say "I do," Dawn's mom and Mary Anne's dad were married, and Dawn and Mary Anne became sisters. But Dawn got homesick for California and made the difficult decision to move back to live with her father and her brother (who had decided to move back earlier). We all stay in touch with her.

Dawn is pretty cool. She's an environmentalist, doesn't eat red meat, and is into the one sport I haven't tried yet — surfing. She is tall and thin, with long, ice-blonde hair and pale blue eyes. She tans easily but gets freckles too.

Stacey McGill is also tall, very thin, and blonde, with pale skin and big blue eyes. She's a math whiz and a fashion maven. She's originally from New York City and goes back often to visit her father, who returned after the McGills got divorced.

Stacey often seems older than the rest of us, perhaps because of her big-city background. Or maybe it's because she has had to take a lot of responsibility for herself since she discovered that she has a disease called diabetes.

When you have diabetes, your body can't handle sugar. Stacey has to be very careful about what she eats (no sweets), and she gives herself daily injections of insulin. But she takes it all in her sophisticated stride.

I think Stacey's style is a reflection of her city background. For instance, today, when we were all dressed warmly and casually, Stacey was wearing a cropped sweater in dark blue-green that looked good with her blue eyes. She also had on a short skirt (black faux suede), pale blue tights, and very cool-looking black suede boots that came to just above her knees. Tiny gold knot earrings completed her ensemble.

The other "ensembled" person in the group is Stacey's best friend, Claudia. As I said, Claudia is veep of the BSC because she has her own phone line — and because she keeps us supplied with huge quantities of junk food that she keeps hidden around her room, from pretzels (for Stacey, since she can't have sugar) to Twinkies and Hershey Hugs (a current favorite of Claud's). Today, she was relying on chocolate trail mix to get her through the meeting, and we were all pitching in to help eat it, except for Stacey, who was eating an apple.

Claudia's ensembles resemble Stacey's only in that they fit her personality and make her stand out from the crowd. Claudia is an artist who struggles in school but has no problem being amazingly creative. She's overshadowed a bit by her older sister, Janine, who has test scores that prove, to the experts at least, that she is a certifiable genius. But I read somewhere recently that IQ tests only measure one kind of genius and that there really are many different kinds of intelligence. Claudia proves it. She is, I believe, an artistic genius.

She's also a knockout, with dark brown eyes, jet-black hair, and a creamy complexion (in spite of all the junk she eats!). She usually dresses like a work of art herself, or as she likes to describe it, a work-in-progress. Today the room was considerably brighter because Claudia had decided to wear red. That meant she had on a red tunic with an orange-red braided belt (that she had made herself, naturally). Her leggings were a rose-pink color, and she had on black shiny flats with tiny rosettes on the toe. She'd pulled her hair back with a large red silk scarf that matched the tunic. Her earrings were silver snowflakes, also homemade. On anybody else, this outfit might have looked overwhelming, but on Claudia it was smashing.

Mallory Pike and Jessica Ramsey are another pair of BSC best friends. Jessi has a younger sister, Becca, and a baby brother, John Philip, Jr., whom everyone calls Squirt. Her aunt Cecelia lives with the family and helps out, the way Nannie does with Kristy's family. Jessi, like Kristy, is organized. Like Claudia, she has artistic ambitions.

In Jessi's case, however, the art is ballet. She wants to be a prima ballerina and gets up *every* morning at 5:29 to practice her ballet moves at the *barre* in her basement. She also takes classes twice a week in Stamford and has even had roles in ballets.

Although Jessi dressed casually for our meeting, you would have guessed she was a ballet dancer by the way she wore her dark hair pulled back in a neat bun, or the way she was (as usual) doing stretches as she sat on the floor, her long arms curving in graceful arcs. Jessi has dark brown eyes and brown skin. She often wears pink or lavender leotards that set off her coloring — and add to her ballet-dancer aura.

No one, on the other hand, would mistake Mallory Pike for a ballet dancer. Although Mal and Jessi are about the same height, Mal is sturdier in build and she usually allows her reddish-brown hair to fall over her shoulders. She has pale skin with a scattering of freckles and, to her eternal despair, wears glasses and braces. I keep telling her glasses are no big deal, but Mallory pines for contact lenses, which she plans to get as soon as she's older. She can't wait to lose her braces either, although they are practically invisible.

Really, Mal can find a dramatic story in almost anything. She wants to be a writer *and* an illustrator when she grows up. She's already won a prize for writing. She's also the babysitter with the most at-home experience. That's because she is the oldest of eight siblings, including triplets. Maybe that contributes to Mal's storytelling abilities. It can't be easy keeping seven brothers and sisters entertained and out of trouble. But somehow Mal manages to do it, and keep calm at the same time.

The ability to keep calm is something that Mallory and Jessi share. They also both love horses and mysteries. Their favorite author is Marguerite Henry.

Shannon goes to a private school, Stoneybrook Day School. Like Kristy, she wears a uniform every day, but in her case, it's a required school uniform. She looks pretty good in it too. She has thick, curly blonde hair, blue eyes, high cheekbones, and wears black mascara every day.

Also like Kristy, Shannon is an Achiever with a capital *A*. She's an excellent student and a member of the Honor Society, the debate team (one of the best in the state), the Astronomy Club, the French Club. In addition to all that, she participates in school plays and was one of the leads in a Drama Club production of *Arsenic and Old Lace*.

It makes even me tired to think about it, but all that activity doesn't seem to faze Shannon, an outstanding quality for a baby-sitter.

Last (but not least, especially for Mary Anne!) is Logan Bruno. Mary Anne thinks Logan looks like her favorite TV star, Cam Geary. I don't know about that, but I admit that with his blue eyes, curly blond-brown hair, and nice athletic build, he's cute. Logan is from Kentucky and has a soft southern accent that I like to listen to. He also has a good sense of humor and *loves* sports (of which I naturally approve). In fact, Logan is as big a sports fanatic as I am, although his sports are track, football, and baseball rather than soccer. And, of course, he is a very good baby-sitter.

Logan and Shannon weren't at the meeting, but the rest of us were. We were all talking at once about the Addisons when we got the first phone call of the day. However, we quieted down as Kristy picked up the phone and said, "The Baby-sitters Club. May I help you? . . . Hi, Mr. Papadakis."

The Papadakises live across the street from Kristy and have been regular clients of the BSC for ages.

Mary Anne took out the record book and got ready to make a note of the appointment. But when Kristy hung up the phone, her first words were, "Guess what? I have more amazing news."

"The Papadakises are moving?" said Claudia, looking unhappy.

"No. Lou McNally is coming back to town."

A stunned silence met this announcement.

21

Then Mary Anne said, with quick sympathy, "Oh, no. Is something wrong? Is Lou all right?"

"She's not in trouble, is she?" asked Mal anxiously.

As you may remember, I mentioned Lou earlier. She had earned the title "Worst Kid Ever" from us during her stay in Stoneybrook. Lou was a foster child and had been placed with the Papadakises after her father died (her mother had been long gone). Her older brother, Jay, had been sent to another foster family.

Baby-sitting for Lou was practically dangerous. You never knew what she was going to do. Her stunts and behavior often incited an all-out war with the other kids around her.

But, as the BSC soon figured out, Lou wasn't really bad. She was unhappy. And who wouldn't be?

Fortunately, Lou's story had a happy ending. Her uncle and aunt were located, and Lou and Jay were reunited in their custody. They even gave Lou a three-month-old black Labrador puppy, whom Lou named Happy, because, as she wrote in a letter to Kristy, "She's happy all the time. Silly dog."

Kristy grinned. "I don't know if Lou has turned into the best kid ever," she said, "but apparently she's doing fine. And now the McNallys are moving to Stoneybrook!"

"That's great!" said Claudia.

22

"Where's their new house?" Stacey asked.

"Near you, Claudia," Kristy answered.

"But the Addisons don't live that close by," I blurted out.

Everyone looked at me in confusion. Then Jessi said, "Oh. Are the McNallys moving into the Addisons' house?"

"I don't think so," said Kristy.

"So we've got *two* new families coming to Stoneybrook," said Stacey.

Kristy gestured with an impatient motion of her hand. "Anyway, Mr. Papadakis wants to set up a sitter for Lou and Jay while the McNallys unpack."

"I'd love to see Lou again," said Claudia. "As long as she's no longer the Worst Kid Ever."

"I agree," said Kristy.

Meanwhile, Mary Anne was running her finger down the list of available sitters. Only one of us could take the job.

Me.

"Lucky Abby," said Jessi, smiling at me.

Maybe yes, maybe no, I thought, but I didn't say anything. I'd wait and see if the Worst Kid Ever still lived up to her name.

CHAPTER 3

Mrs. Bernhardt, my history teacher, is short and big-chested, with thick, curly blonde hair, and smiles a lot through the ton of makeup she inevitably wears. She is also known as Dolly One. Dolly Two is Ms. Vandela, another short, big-chested blonde teacher with a fondness for heavy-duty cosmetics. Their real names are not Dolly, but both are Dolly Parton look-alikes and *huge* Dolly Parton fans.

Dolly One, Dolly Two. Hmmm. Sounds like the title to a country-western song, doesn't it?

Don't get me wrong. I like Dolly One (I've never had a class with Dolly Two). She may smile more than your average human being, but I think most of the time it's sincere. However, history is not my best subject. I guess I take it places where it doesn't necessarily want to go. . . .

Mrs. Bernhardt didn't quite know what to do when I suggested that since Philadelphia was the City of Brotherly Love, we ought to have a city named Philasororia (for the City of Sisterly Love). And she didn't even laugh when I said that if we couldn't name a city that, it would make a great name for a dinosaur.

Sometimes I see Mrs. Bernhardt looking at me as if I were the Student from Another Planet.

But she did manage a smile when I stopped by her desk after school that Tuesday.

"Abigail, how are you, honey?" she asked.

I'd been sitting in her class for the last fifty minutes, so you'd think she'd already know. But that's the way Mrs. Bernhardt is.

"Fine, thank you," I said. "Except for my grade."

With a look of distress, Mrs. Bernhardt said, "Well, I know your grades aren't what they should be. What are we going to *do* about it?"

"We?" I said.

Mrs. Bernhardt raised her eyebrows. She might have a soft exterior and syrupy voice, but underneath, she is steely to the bone.

Moving right along, I said, "Well, I'd like to bring my grade up, of course. So I thought we could talk about the Black History Month projects."

"Ah, yes. We have quite a few topics to choose from." Mrs. B reached into her top drawer and pulled out a folder. She opened it and extracted two sheets of paper stapled together at the top.

I recognized the handout material we'd been given when the projects had been announced. "I've been thinking about Black History Month education," I said. "What I'd like to do is help some of the neighborhood kids do a project for the big presentation at the Stoneybrook Community Center."

"I'm not sure I understand," said Mrs. Bernhardt.

"I'll help organize the project," I said. "And I'll also document how the different kids work together. You know, it'll be a project within a project. Two for the price of one. Double the fun. Twofers."

Holding up one scarlet-nailed hand, Mrs. Bernhardt said, "I get your drift. But I'm not sure you realize how much work you are proposing to take on. I don't want a shoddy presentation. . . ."

"It won't be!" I said, stung. I mean, I wasn't Mrs. B's best student, but I wasn't a slacker either. "It'll be the best project this class has ever seen."

"Well," said Mrs. Bernhardt. She tapped one red nail against her lipsticked lips. "All right. But if you turn in a bad project, it won't help your grade, Abigail."

"No problem," I said.

Claudia and Stacey, who are in my class, had waited for me in the hall.

"How'd it go?" Stacey asked.

Claudia patted my arm as if to console me. Since she's not a good student, Claudia doesn't like even the *thought* of having a conference with a teacher — not even a voluntary one.

I gave Claud a reassuring smile and told them both, "Easy as pie."

"Pi?" said Stacey. "R squared?"

"Pie?" asked Claudia. "What flavor?"

I knew Stacey was talking math and Claudia was talking junk food. I laughed, and they laughed too.

"Easy," I said. "She agreed to it."

"So what's your project going to be on?" asked Claudia.

"Well, I haven't quite finalized my plans yet," I answered. "I'll let you know as soon as I do."

"Good," said Stacey. "We'll help you out."

Claudia nodded and we parted ways to go to our next classes. I was relieved that they hadn't asked more questions.

Why?

Because although I had told Mrs. Bernhardt "No problem," of course there was a problem. Mrs. Bernhardt had sensed it too.

I had my presentation worked out, but I didn't have the subject. I mean, what was my project going to be about? I had no idea.

I went into project mode for the rest of the day. I thought about it in math. I thought about it in English. I thought about it in gym. Little bitty pieces of ideas would float to the surface. I thought of people worthy of a project: Wilma Rudolph. Sojourner Truth. Rosa Parks.

But how could I develop any of this into something that would meet Mrs. Bernhardt's standards? Plus, I was pretty sure that lots of my ideas had already been claimed by other students.

I'd have to think of something, and fast. Otherwise my grade would ruin my social life . . . by getting me seriously grounded.

CHAPTER 4

"Hi, I'm Mr. McNally. You must be Abby."

I nodded and shook hands with the short, dark-haired man who'd opened the door. He was wiry, with a brisk manner and a kind face. "The movers will be here tomorrow," he explained as he led me down a hallway. "We're staying in a motel tonight, but we've brought over a few carloads that we're trying to get unpacked now."

"We still have boxes we haven't unpacked from when *we* moved to Stoneybrook," I said.

Mr. NcNally smiled. "Don't tell Sarabeth," he said. Before I could ask who Sarabeth was, Mr. McNally said, "Sarabeth, Abby's here."

A tall woman with laugh lines at the corners of her green eyes turned and looked down at me from a step stool by a kitchen cabinet. An open box of dishes told me what she'd been doing. "Hi," she said. "I'm Sarabeth McNally. Welcome to our mess!"

At that moment, a gravelly voice said, "You're not Kristy."

I turned and saw a small, wiry girl standing in the doorway. I knew it had to be Lou McNally. "No," I said. "I'm Abby. I'm the newest member of the Baby-sitters Club." Then I added reassuringly, "Kristy sent me."

The girl walked forward and held out her hand, just as her uncle had done. "How do you do," she said formally. "I'm Louisa McNally. I'm sorry if I was rude."

I was surprised. "You weren't rude," I said.

A taller boy had followed Lou into the kitchen. He said, "Hi, I'm Jay. Are you our baby-sitter?"

"Yes."

"I'm eleven and I don't need a baby-sitter."

Lou grabbed the sleeve of Jay's flannel shirt and tugged it. "Jay!" she exclaimed in an agonized whisper. "That's not nice."

"No problem," I said.

Mr. McNally said, "Well, you don't have to think of Abby as a baby-sitter, but she is in charge of you two right now, okay?"

I had been prepared for Jay to argue or scowl. But he just shrugged and said, "Okay."

"Isn't someone missing?" I asked. "I thought I'd get to meet a terrific dog named Happy McNally too."

"I just let her out into the backyard for a little

while," said Lou. "I didn't want her to mess up the house."

Mrs. McNally smiled. "You don't want to leave her outside too long, dear. It's cold."

"I'll get her!" cried Jay, and he ran to the back door and threw it open. The black Labrador puppy bounded in. As I bent over to say hello, she leaped up and licked me on the chin, her tail whirling like a helicopter's blades.

"Happy!" said Lou in a worried voice. "Off!" Happy flattened her ears and slid down onto her front paws.

"She's adorable," I said, and sneezed. Uh-oh. My allergies were kicking in. Quickly I added, "Why don't we take Happy for a walk? I'll show you the neighborhood."

"If that's what you would like to do," said Lou. She glanced toward her aunt and uncle. "And if it's okay with Aunt Sarabeth and Uncle Mac."

"Sure," said her uncle. "Have fun and stay out of trouble."

Lou's cheeks reddened. She said solemnly, "I won't get into any trouble. I promise."

I helped Lou and Jay into their coats. Then I buttoned mine up again and fastened the leash to Happy's collar. We walked outside and Jay said, "Let me walk Happy."

"Abby can walk her," said Lou.

Jay looked as if he were going to argue. Then he said, "Well, Happy's your dog. I guess so. . . ."

"If you don't mind, Lou, I don't mind if Jay walks her."

"Okay," said Lou.

Jay grabbed the leash, looped it around his wrist, and said, "Come on, girl!" The two of them took off, sprinting down the sidewalk.

Lou walked sedately by my side. "This looks like a nice neighborhood," she said.

"It is. And I think you already know one of your neighbors, Mary Anne Spier."

"Oh. Yes. I remember," said Lou. "How is Mary Anne?"

She sounded just like a miniature adult — and *so* serious.

"She's fine," I said.

"The sidewalk ends!" exclaimed Jay. "Just like that! We live in the neighborhood where the sidewalk ends!"

"Just like in the book," I agreed.

Jay looked pleased. "Do you know that book? *Where the Sidewalk Ends*? It's great!"

"It's funny too. Do you like it, Lou?"

Lou smiled. "It's an interesting book," she said.

We reached the end of the sidewalk and I pointed. "That's Mary Anne's house, up that hill."

"Burnt Hill Road," Jay read from the sign-post.

"I'm not sure why it's called that," I said. "It's an odd name, isn't it?"

Happy took a bite of snow, snorted, and shook her head. Her ears flapped and both Lou and Jay laughed.

"Beyond Mary Anne's house is a farm where a goose named Screaming Yellow Honker lives. We'll visit there sometime. There's also a goat named Elvira."

"Cool," Jay exclaimed.

"I've never met a goat or a goose," said Lou.

"You'll like them," I promised her. "Also, another one of Mary Anne's neighbors, Mrs. Towne, makes beautiful quilts. I'm sure Mary Anne will introduce you to her too."

"Let's visit the farm now!" Jay cried.

"It's too icy on the edge of the road," I replied. "I don't think it's safe to walk there. We'd better stick to the sidewalks."

Jay made a face. But he didn't argue as we turned around and walked in the other direction.

A huge dog came bounding out to the fence in one front yard, barking loudly. Jay jumped back and Happy jumped forward, pressing her nose to the posts.

"Happy, no!" screamed Lou, her eyes wide. She tore her hand loose from mine and hurled herself forward to protect Happy. Then she stopped as the two dogs sniffed noses and wagged their tails.

Jay put his hand on his sister's shoulder. "You worry too much," he said gently. "It's okay, see? They're making friends."

Lou nodded.

Jay started to run along the sidewalk again. Lou said, "Jay, be careful. What if there are other dogs and they're big and mean?"

"We'll be fine," Jay assured her. "We're just going to the end of the block." He glanced at me and I nodded.

"Go ahead," I said. To Lou I suggested, "Let's watch. It'll be okay."

Jay shot me a relieved look and raced ahead. Lou kept walking sedately next to me.

When Jay and Happy returned, they were both panting. Jay said, "Come on, Lou. It's fun. Happy loves to run!"

Lou shook her head. "I might fall and get dirty."

"A little dirt never hurts," I observed.

But Lou wouldn't budge. So Jay took off again as we reached the next block. That suited Happy just fine, since she was full of puppy energy. In fact, I guess you could say that they were *both* full of puppy energy.

Meanwhile, Lou was a model child. She asked questions about the neighborhood and the school. She talked to me about soccer (I saw her eyes brighten when I offered to give her some soccer lessons). She was amazingly unlike the bad kid I'd been led to expect. I began to wonder if the BSC members had been overreacting.

We returned to find Mr. and Mrs. McNally just finishing up.

"Did you have a nice walk?" Mrs. McNally asked.

Jay, his cheeks red with cold, said, "It was great."

Lou said, "I enjoyed it very much. Thank you, Abby. I'll get Happy a bowl of water."

Mr. McNally handed Lou a bowl, which she filled. "Would you like some water too?" she asked me.

I shook my head, but Jay said, "I would!"

Carefully, Lou filled a glass of water. She turned to hand it to Jay and somehow dropped it. It hit the floor and bounced (it was plastic). Water splashed everywhere. Some of it hit Happy, who gave a yip of surprise and jumped back, turning over her own water bowl.

In two seconds flat, the floor of the kitchen resembled a small lake.

"Oh, no," said Lou. "I'm sorry! I didn't mean to. It was an accident. I'll clean it up right away!"

"Of course it was an accident," her aunt said

soothingly. Mr. McNally had already gotten a mop from the utility closet next to the back door and begun mopping up the water.

"I'll do that," said Lou.

"It's okay, Lou," he said.

The water was mopped up almost as quickly as it had been spilled, but Lou kept apologizing. "It wasn't Happy's fault," she insisted. "But I didn't mean to do it. I'm really, really sorry."

"Chill, Lou," said Jay, giving her a grin and a punch on the arm. "Maybe we won't have to take baths tonight."

"And maybe you will," said Mrs. McNally, laughing.

Lou didn't laugh.

Mr. McNally said, "Well, I guess we've done all we can do today. Let's get back to the motel."

"Can we give you a ride home, Abby?" Mrs. McNally asked.

"That'd be great," I answered.

So the McNallys drove me home. As I got out of the car, Jay said, "See you later, alligator."

"In awhile, crocodile," I answered.

Jay laughed as if I'd said the funniest thing ever, and Mr. and Mrs. McNally grinned.

But Lou only smiled a small smile and said, "Thank you, Abby."

"You're welcome, Lou," I answered. I waved as they drove away. I couldn't wait to tell my friends the news. Lou McNally, the Worst Kid Ever, had somehow been magically transformed into the Princess of Perfect.

CHAPTER 5

Friday

I didn't know it was going to be so hard to say goodby to Carrie and Shean. Espeshially Carrie. And you know what else was strange. The whole time I was babysiting for them while everthing was geting packed up I kept thinking about mimi.

"Hey, hey, hey," Claudia greeted Corrie Addison.

Corrie looked up and smiled happily. "Claudia!" she cried.

"Corrie, my main artist. How are you doing?"

"I'm packing," she said.

"Are you sure you're not unpacking?" Claudia teased. "That's a lot of stuff you have scattered around."

It was true. Every drawer in Corrie's dresser was open. Clothes, shoes, books, and toys were piled in a crazy heap on the bed. Her garbage can was overflowing and next to it was a bulging trash bag. Half-filled boxes lined the room.

But then the whole house was like that. It was hard to believe that the Addisons would be ready to move on time. Claudia couldn't imagine trying to pack up everything she owned. In fact, she had trouble packing for sleepovers.

Corrie made a face. "I don't want to move," she said. "I've lived in Stoneybrook nine whole years. My whole life."

"Me too," Claudia echoed. "I mean, I've lived here my whole life too. It would be very hard to move."

"I'll miss all my friends." Corrie sighed. And you too, Claudia."

"I'll miss you," Claudia said, feeling a sudden sharp pang. It wasn't just for Corrie. It was because at that moment she realized that she connected Corrie with her own grandmother, Mimi. Claudia had been giving Corrie art lessons when Mimi became sick and died.

Mimi, thought Claudia. *My grandmother, my first and best friend in the whole world.* She blinked quickly to keep tears from filling her eyes and said, "But you know what? I'm not going to stay in Stoneybrook my whole life. I'm going to leave in just a few years to become a famous artist."

"Where will you go to do that?" asked Corrie.

"Paris. New York. I haven't made up my mind," Claudia said.

"When *I* become a famous artist, maybe we'll live in the same city," said Corrie.

"Or even have artwork in the same galleries and museums," Claudia added.

Corrie was looking more cheerful. Then she glanced around her room again and sighed. "But I still have to pack."

"Not right away," Claudia said, assigning packing to the same status she assigned homework. "I have a better idea."

"What?"

"Why don't we make a picture of Stoneybrook, a map of the places you like and special things that have happened to you so you won't forget. You can take it with you and hang it in your new room."

"Yes!" Corrie cried.

Corrie had several enormous pieces of poster board for her various art projects. She and Claudia chose the biggest and put it on the floor.

"We could ask Sean to help," Claudia said.

Corrie shrugged. "He's pretty cranky, but you can try."

Corrie was right. Sean *was* pretty cranky. "No, I don't want to work on a stupid poster. I do that in school," he said.

"This is not a school project," Claudia told him indignantly.

But Sean just shook his head. "I have my own work to do. Do you mind?"

"Okay." Claudia backed off. "We'll be in Corrie's room if you change your mind."

"I won't."

Claudia joined Corrie again, a tiny bit relieved that she wouldn't have to deal with Sean in his difficult state.

Corrie found the Stoneybrook phone book and she and Claudia drew a map of Stoneybrook based on the map in the front of the book. It wasn't an exact replica, but it was a start.

"What's that?" Claudia asked, after they'd been working a few minutes.

Corrie gave Claudia a sly glance. "It's Stoneybrook Elementary School," she said. "And that little tiny building near it is Stoneybrook Middle School."

Claudia had to laugh. For once, the elementary school was bigger than the middle school.

Next, Claudia drew a letter carrier handing out mail. Corrie added a dog barking at the letter carrier.

Then Corrie drew a picture of a house on fire. "That happened to my best friend in kindergarten," she explained. "But everything turned out okay."

They used fluorescent paint to make the flames shooting out of the windows and silver glitter for the water coming from the firefighters' hoses.

Then Corrie drew a tiny figure holding a paintbrush, standing outside her house.

"Who's that?" asked Claudia.

"You," said Corrie. She studied Claudia for a moment and said, "Could I cut off a tiny piece of your hair?"

Claudia thought it over and said, "Okay."

Very carefully, Corrie snipped a smidgen of hair from Claudia's ponytail. As Claudia watched, Corrie glued the hair to the tiny figure with the paintbrush.

"Excellent," said Claudia. "Now I'll draw a picture of you."

She put Corrie on the front steps of the Stoneybrook Museum, carrying an enormous painting. Then she snipped a tiny bit of Corrie's hair and added it to the figure.

For the next piece of the map, Corrie decided to use some of the plastic figures from her old collection of farm animals. She and Claudia put a goat in a pen by a barn near Mary Anne's house. They added a horse grazing on Jessi's lawn and another one on Mal's front porch, since they both like horses so much. They put a drawing of Kristy's grandmother's pink car (which everyone calls the Pink Clinker) on Main Street, with flowers falling out of the windows, pursued by a Stoneybrook police officer.

By the time Claudia had to leave, Corrie's Portrait of Stoneybrook had gone from serious to outrageous.

Even Sean admired it, in his own way, when he came in to see why Claudia and Corrie were laughing so hard.

"Hey," he said, "cool." And with Corrie and

Claudia's help, he added himself on his skateboard, with puffs of smoke trailing behind him (to show how fast he was going).

Right before Claudia left, she sat back and surveyed the collage/mural/found-art piece.

"This," she said, "isn't just cool. It's extremely cool."

She knew Mimi would agree.

CHAPTER 6

Mrs. Papadakis came bustling through the front door of the McNallys' new house, carrying not one but two enormous thermoses. Behind her, Linny (age nine) and Hannie (age seven) were lugging a huge cooler between them. Bringing up the rear was Mr. Papadakis with Sari (age two) in one arm and a picnic basket in the other.

"Good," Mrs. Papadakis declared. "We beat the movers."

"Are we going to have a picnic?" Jay asked.

"A breakfast picnic," Hannie replied.

"I'll hold Sari," I said, and lifted Sari from Mr. Papadakis's arms. She smiled at me and seemed content to watch all the hustle and bustle around her.

It was move-in day for the McNallys and I had just arrived. My mission? To help the parents take care of Linny, Hannie, Sari, Lou, and Jay when the Amazon Moving Company showed up. (Happy had been put into the kennel at the veterinarian's for the day. The McNallys would get her that night, after everything was moved in.) Although the movers were supposed to be at the McNallys' new house at 8:00 A.M., they hadn't arrived yet.

As I bounced Sari gently on my hip, the Papadakises unpacked a breakfast feast: bagels, cream cheese, jam, fresh fruit, and even cereal, milk, and juice. The two thermoses contained regular and decaffeinated coffee.

"This is wonderful," said Mrs. McNally as Mr. Papadakis unfolded a large tablecloth from over his arm and spread it out ceremoniously on the kitchen floor.

"Well, we can't help you move in if we don't all have a good, nourishing breakfast," said Mr. Papadakis.

Everyone sat down on the floor and began to talk and laugh over the breakfast "picnic."

Hannie had taken a seat next to Lou. As I watched, Hannie spread jam on the two halves of a bagel and offered one of them to Lou.

"Thank you," said Lou.

"You're welcome," said Hannie. She gave Lou a tentative smile, and I remembered that the relationship between Lou and Hannie had been a difficult one, although they had parted on friendly terms.

Lou smiled back, even more tentatively. She took a bite of a bagel and a dollop of jam dropped off onto her pale orange T-shirt.

"Uh-oh," said Hannie, pointing.

Lou leaped up. "Oh! Oh, I'm sorry," she cried. She looked wildly across the table at her aunt.

Mrs. McNally said, "Just wash it off, Lou. It's an old T-shirt and I expect it will get a lot dirtier than that before moving day is over."

"I will. I'm sorry, I'm sorry," Lou apologized, dashing out of the kitchen.

A few minutes later, after Lou had returned with a big wet spot on her shirt and had switched to a bagel with no jam, the doorbell rang. The movers had arrived.

From then on, it was chaos. Linny and Jay organized a box relay. Hannie opened and closed doors for the movers. I went out to the Papadakises' car to get Sari's portable playpen and set it up in a corner of the den, where I could keep an eye on her without getting in the way.

Mr. and Mrs. McNally took turns standing by the front door with a list, reading the numbers and labels on boxes and directing them to different rooms.

It seemed that whenever I turned around, Lou was there, offering to help. She cleared the remnants of the picnic from the kitchen. She set potted plants in windows. And when she accidentally dropped a box, she almost burst into tears.

"It's okay, Lou," I said.

Her eyes were huge in her thin face. "I didn't mean it," she said with a gasp. "You won't tell?"

"What's to tell? It was a box of kitchen utensils. It made a nice clatter, but nothing got broken." I opened the box (which was labeled KITCHEN UTENSILS) and showed Lou. She seemed slightly reassured but not all that happy.

A moment later a familiar voice said, "At the rate everything's going, you guys are going to be moved in by lunchtime."

"Maybe not lunchtime," I said. "Hi, Stacey. Hi, Jackie. Hi, Shea. Where's Archie?" Stacey was baby-sitting for the Rodowskys that day: Shea is nine and Jackie is seven (and known as "the Walking Disaster" because of his ability to get into amazing and often hilarious mishaps). Archie is four.

"Mom took him to get new snow boots," said Shea. "He lost one of his others." Shea and Jackie exchanged a glance, and I had a feeling they knew more about the missing snow boot than either of them was telling. I decided not to pursue it.

"How's it going?" Stacey asked.

"It's going," I said, just as two movers staggered by with a large overstuffed chair. "Left," the woman grunted. "Up. Left." The chair disappeared down the hall.

"That's Uncle Mac's chair," said Jay. "I better go make sure they put it in the right place in the den."

"I'll help," said Lou.

"Little Miss Perfect," teased Jay.

Lou smiled at her brother and bustled after him. She turned at the door to say, "I'm glad to see you again, Stacey."

Stacey raised an eyebrow. "Where's the real Lou?" she said after Lou had left.

"As far as I know, this is the real Lou," I said. "She's been like this ever since I met her. I told you she wasn't anything like the Louisa McNally you guys had described to me."

"You're not kidding. If I hadn't met her before, I wouldn't think it was the same person."

Stacey, Jackie, and Shea pitched in to help. Although Jackie managed to fall over a chair, drop a box of books down the stairs, and get accidentally locked in a closet, no serious mishaps occurred.

When I next saw Lou, she was standing beside her aunt, trying to take an enormous box from her hands. "I can carry it," Lou was saying.

"Lou, dear, it's much too heavy. But thank you."

"No, really, I . . ."

Mrs. McNally looked up and saw me. "Abby," she said, "I've got an idea. Why don't you take the kids out for awhile. I don't think it's too cold. Besides, we're getting to the big furniture and frankly, I could use a little breathing room."

"Sure," I said, grinning at the sudden image of Jackie somehow getting folded up in a sofa.

Mr. Papadakis stuck his head around the edge of the door. "I'll keep an eye on Sari," he added.

"Great," I said.

Meanwhile, Lou had dropped her hands from the box she'd been trying to tug out of her aunt's arms. She stood there for a moment, her hands hanging limply at her sides, her face oddly pale. Then she turned and rushed away.

I found Stacey, who suggested we take everyone to the Stoneybrook Elementary School playground. The idea was an instant hit with everyone, except possibly Lou. She didn't say anything. She just put on her coat, gloves, and knit cap and stood silently by the door.

When we walked outside, she slipped her hand into mine, still without speaking.

At the playground, we ran into Mal and her brothers — the ten-year-old triplets, Byron, Jordan, and Adam, and eight-year-old Nicky — playing kickball. In no time at all, a large, energetic game had developed. I was glad to see Lou jump into the fray with the rest of the kids. I couldn't help but notice how protective of her Jay was, something I suspected he had long been.

My spirits fell a little when Lou quit the game abruptly a few minutes later. She tried to catch a ball that Adam had kicked, but she missed and wound up with a streak of mud along the arm of her coat. She then danced up and down, shaking her arm as if something had bitten her, crying, "It's dirty, it's dirty."

Everyone looked surprised. After all, while we weren't at the playground to get deliberately dirty, it went with the territory.

"It's okay, Lou," I said, wiping most of the mud off with my mitten. But she didn't seem to be comforted. And she didn't return to the kickball game. She stood between me and Stacey and simply watched.

It was then that a lightbulb went on in my head. I was looking at the gathering of kids and thinking about the Black History Month project. I was completely stumped for ideas. Maybe the kids could help. They were beginning to look tired and cold anyway.

51

I pulled off one glove, put my fingers in my mouth, and blew a piercing whistle. "Okay, everybody, I'm calling a special Saturday SES playground assembly! Listen up."

They all gathered around, even Stacey and Mal.

"This is the deal," I said. "I need help with a project for school. I may also need a few volunteers."

"What project?" asked Hannie.

"For Black History Month," I said. That produced nods of recognition. "But I don't know yet what my project is going to be about."

"Kwanzaa," said Linny. "We studied that in school in December. It's a cool holiday. You could do your project on that."

"It's a good idea. But like you, most kids just finished studying Kwanzaa. I don't think my teacher will go for the idea."

Linny nodded, looking thoughtful.

"What about sports?" Mal asked. "You're a sports fan. You could do a project on Wilma Rudolph and Jesse Owens."

"Or the Negro Baseball Leagues," said Jay.

I thought about that. It sounded good.

Then Nicky shouted, "No! Do the Underground Railroad. Do Mary Anne's house!"

It was a brilliantly simple, simply brilliant idea. I stared at Nicky, openmouthed, then said, "That's it! Nicky, you're a genius."

Nicky beamed.

Mal said, "Way to go, Nick."

Mary Anne's house is believed by some people to be haunted, in part because of the secret passage beneath it. The house was built in 1795 and used to be a stop on the Underground Railroad, which helped to smuggle slaves into the free North before the Civil War.

Lou pulled on my arm. "What about Mary Anne's house?"

A cold gust of wind blew and I decided we'd all been outside long enough. "Let's head back to your house, Lou, and I'll explain."

So as we walked home, I told Lou and Jay the story of the secret passage.

"I'll help with your project," Lou volunteered. "I can do lots of work. I'll be really good and work really, really hard."

I was pleased by Lou's enthusiasm. She'd seemed so reserved up until now. "That'd be great," I said.

"You'll let me?" she asked.

"Silly," said Jay. "Abby wants us all to help, don't you?"

"Yup. Lou and you and everybody."

"Wait until we tell Aunt Sarabeth and Uncle Mac that we're helping Abby on a big, important middle-school project." Lou gave a little skip and I hid a smile.

A big, important middle-school project?

Well, it was pretty big and important to me. I gave Lou's hand a squeeze. This project was going to be a winner. I had a very good feeling about it.

And no idea of all the trouble that lay ahead.

CHAPTER 7

Stoneybrook is rich in history.

If that sounds like the opening line of a project, that's because it is. One of several I had in mind.

Unfortunately, the more research I did at the library and at the Stoneybrook Historical Society, the more it became clear that an opening line was the least of my worries. I mean, there are volumes and *volumes* of information about the Underground Railroad. Should I focus on Harriet Tubman, who had been one of the most famous members of the Underground Railroad? I decided against that, although she was certainly a very important part of it. But I was sure that other projects would have the same focus, and I didn't think duplicating someone else's material would impress Dolly One.

What about the daring escapes, like that of Henry Box Brown, who'd mailed himself to freedom in a box so small no one was suspicious of it? That had possibilities, but I didn't think I had the capacity to film the escape, and if I didn't film it, it would sound like just another book report to Dolly One. I was sure of that. The project would have to have something extra.

Maybe I could create an Underground Railroad map of Stoneybrook. It was a crossroads for one of the smaller lines of the Underground Railroad, sending fugitives north to Canada in a couple of directions. Not only that, but Abigail Grey, a leading abolitionist and Quaker, had been a resident of Stoneybrook and was suspected of being a Railroad stationmaster.

I was amazed and awed. And the more I read, the harder it became to narrow the subject. Not only did I feel pressure to make it the best project ever, but I also felt I could not do a disservice to such an important topic by turning in a crummy report.

By this time, Vanessa, Margo, and Claire Pike had also volunteered to be part of the project, which made thirteen kids in all, not including my fellow BSC members. I had enough volunteers. All I needed was something for them to do.

Time was passing far too quickly.

I finally decided on one thing. I was going to document my project on video. We have a

56

video camera that is small and easy to use, so that was no problem.

I called a meeting of the "Railroad Project," and we gathered at my house, along with Mal, Jessi, Stacey, and Claudia. When I announced the video idea, everyone was instantly enthusiastic.

"We can write a play! Hooray!" said Vanessa Pike. (She's nine and plans to become a poet. She practices rhyming whenever possible.)

"I want to be a star," Adam proclaimed.

"Me too," Byron and Jordan chimed in.

"We could have a scary chase scene," suggested Hannie. "We studied the Underground Railroad in school. One slave escaped by walking across chunks of ice in a freezing river — while she was holding her baby!"

I knew who Hannie envisioned starring in *that* scene.

Jay said, "Well, we can find a river and float blocks of ice in it. That would make it really real."

"Wait a minute, wait a minute." I tried to calm the kids down. "We need to do more research before we make any decisions."

That's when I had a brilliant idea. I'd document the process of making the decision.

As everyone started talking again, I held up my hands. "This is the deal," I explained. "We're going to take a walk to the library. I want everybody to do some research: check out books, look up articles, even read the encyclopedia. Then at our next meeting, we're going to talk about what we learned."

I glanced at Claudia, Stacey, and Mal, who nodded. We bundled everyone up and set out for the library.

The cool thing about the Stoneybrook Public Library (one of many) is that if you walk in one afternoon with thirteen kids who all want to do research on the same subject, the librarians take it in stride. Ms. Feld, the children's librarian, bustled up to us with a big smile. In no time at all she had sorted us into groups by reading level. Soon the kids were up to their eyeballs, almost literally, in books, magazines, and reference materials.

Claudia said, "I'm going to work on visuals. Even if you don't know what you're going to do yet, you're going to need titles. I was thinking I could do something with kente cloth." She went in search of art books that might feature the traditional African pattern material. Mal set to work on her own project, which she described as a "deconstruction of *Uncle Tom's Cabin* from 1852 until now." It sounded impressive and made me more than a little worried about what I was going to do. Stacey found a book called *Finances for Dummies* and kept an eye on the kids while she turned pages and guffawed as if she were reading the funniest joke book ever.

After about twenty minutes of card catalog research and stack wandering I had an armful of books. I paged through all of them carefully, putting the ones I wanted to check out in a neat pile on one corner of the table and the ones I didn't need right away on the chair next to me. I had just finished separating the books I wanted from the ones I didn't when Lou appeared at my elbow. "Can I help you with something?" she asked.

"Maybe. I've got to look up some other books on Stoneybrook history and some more stuff about the Underground Railroad."

A quick scroll through the computer card file gave me a new list of books. With Lou at my heels, I went into the stacks and began to pull more books from the shelves. Lou insisted on holding them.

One book wasn't where it was supposed to be, although the computer had shown that it was not checked out. I squatted down and ran my finger across the shelf of books to make sure that it hadn't been put back out of order. But I could find no sign of *Get on Board, The Story of the Underground Railroad*, by Jim Haskins.

"It's *got* to be here," I muttered.

"I could go ask Ms. Feld," Lou volunteered.

"Good idea," I said. "But put all those books down first before you drop them."

"I won't drop them, I promise," Lou said quickly, but she set the books down and hurried away.

A minute later Lou came hurrying back. "Ms. Feld said that sometimes books have been returned but they haven't yet been put back on the shelf. We should check and see if there are any library carts nearby that might have the one we want."

She looked around and exclaimed, "There's one. Which book was it?"

I told her and a moment later she was pointing triumphantly. "Here it is," she said.

I don't know what happened next. I do know that Lou pulled the book off the library cart — and the cart toppled over with a huge crash. Books cascaded around her legs and her face turned bright red.

"Lou! Are you all right?" I exclaimed.

Ms. Feld appeared at the end of the stack. "Oh, dear! I hope no one is hurt."

Dropping to her knees, Lou began to scrabble frantically among the books. "It was an accident," she said. "I didn't mean to do it, honest. I promise. An accident."

"Of course it was," said Ms. Feld. "No harm done. Let's just get this cart up and put the books back on it."

She matched her actions to her words and, with Lou's almost feverish help, had soon restored the books to the cart.

"Someone will come along and put these in the right order and shelve them a little later. Did you find your book?" Ms. Feld asked.

Lou's hands clenched into fists. "Uh-oh," she said. "I guess I . . . I put it back on the cart."

"Well, it won't be hard to find," I said. I moved quickly between Lou and the cart, before she could help me. "Why don't you take the books I've already picked out back to my table for me? That would be a big help."

Lou nodded and hurried away. I quickly found the book and followed her.

Signs of restlessness in the troops (the triplets were spending their money making photocopies of their faces) alerted me to the fact that it was time to go.

"Let's head out," I said to Mal.

I went to my table to gather up my books, then stopped. The new books I had picked out were all there, neatly stacked up. But all the other ones I had been looking at were gone!

"Oh, no."

Stacey looked up. "What?"

"Did a librarian come along and put away the books I had on the table?"

"No. Lou did. I thought that's what you asked her to do."

"No! She must have misunderstood." I groaned. "We're leaving now and I *need* those books."

Claudia returned in time to overhear our conversation. "We'll take everybody home," she said. "You can look up the books again."

"Thanks, Claud. I owe you."

Claudia grinned. "I don't want much. Just a credit in your documentary."

Lou came running to me. "There are your books," she said. "I put the others away."

"Thanks," I said. What else could I say?

"Come on," Claudia said. "It's time to go."

Mallory and the Pikes were already heading for the exit. Mal signaled to us to hurry up, and I could tell that the Pikes had reached their limit, at least when it came to library time.

"What about you?" Lou asked. "Aren't you coming?"

"I'll catch up with you later," I answered. "I still have research to do."

I waved as everyone left the library. Then, with a weary sigh, I began to duplicate the work I'd done earlier. I didn't have time for mistakes like this, I thought. Lou was trying to be helpful, but she was turning into a one-kid wrecking crew.

And I still didn't have a clue as to what the project was going to be about.

CHAPTER 8

"Keep talking, keep talking," I urged.

Adam Pike stood up and bowed. "My name is Adam Pike." He turned and stared straight into the camera and grinned a big, fake grin.

"Cut, cut, *cut!*" I cried, switching the camera off.

"What? What's wrong?" Adam asked.

"You're supposed to act natural," I said. "This is a documentary, not Hollywood."

"I *am* acting natural."

"Ha!" hooted Byron. "Then why are you introducing yourself to people you already know?"

"I'm not. I'm introducing myself to my audience," Adam answered.

"Forget about the audience," Mal advised. "Just be yourself."

"Oooh, boo," Vanessa said.

"Adam, *awful*," Jordan said.

Adam made a hideous face and sat down.

"Okay, let's try again," I said. "We're discussing our research and talking about some of the things we've learned while we decide where to go with this project. Ready? Go."

Silence.

More silence.

I clicked off the camera. "You guys," I said. "Come on. All you have to do is *talk*."

"What do you want us to say?" asked Linny Papadakis, who was sitting next to Jay.

"Talk about what interests you," I said.

"Anything?" asked Hannie.

"About the Underground Railroad," I amended.

Lou raised her hand as if she were in school.

"Go ahead, Lou," I said.

"Thank you," she said. She lowered her hand. "I'll go first."

"Great! Thanks, Lou."

I reset the camera. Lou cleared her throat and then said, "Stoneybrook was one of the stops on the Underground Railroad. I didn't know that, because I just moved to Stoneybrook."

"You lived in Stoneybrook before," said Hannie.

Lou smiled, almost normally. "I was visiting," she said.

"It wasn't really a railroad," said Nicky. "It was just called that."

"Why?" I asked quickly.

Several people began to talk at once. "One at a time," Kristy reminded them.

After that, everyone seemed to forget about the camera. The discussion ranged far and wide, from the stories of wagons with false bottoms that had been used to transport the fugitives to freedom, to an argument over what the best disguise would be (initiated, naturally, by the Pike triplets).

It was the second meeting of the Railroad Project, held at my house with help from Mal, who'd brought her brothers and sisters, and Kristy, who'd come over with the McNallys and the Papadakises.

I couldn't have gotten even this far without the help of the other BSC members, who were on hand and injected a little order into the potential chaos. However, I couldn't help but feel that Kristy, our fearless leader and Most Organized Person on the Planet, was being, well, just a little judgmental.

Was it something she said? No. It was all the things she *didn't* say. She was uncharacteristically short on suggestions. She didn't even attempt to rearrange everything to suit her idea of efficiency.

Normally, I would have been glad, but now it was making me nervous. What did Kristy know that I didn't? What did she think I was missing?

Besides a focus for my project, of course. I still hadn't narrowed the subject down. And apart from the video documentation, I still hadn't chosen a format.

But it would come to me, I reassured myself. Therefore, I resolutely ignored Kristy's tactful silence.

"Low-battery break," I announced when I saw the camera had run down.

"Empty-stomach break," Jay said.

"It's your lucky day," Kristy proclaimed. "We're making popcorn." (We'd arranged this before.) "Who wants to help?"

You know the answer, right?

Everyone.

So we all trooped into the kitchen. Even though it was my kitchen, Kristy took charge, handing out chores and aprons like a master chef/drill sergeant. I think she was relieved to be in control again.

Making popcorn didn't involve just popping the popcorn in a microwave. It also involved putting "good stuff" on it, as Nicky said. This involved raisins, cinnamon, brown sugar, peanuts, and even nonpareils. (It's not as weird as it sounds.)

As I helped Vanessa and Nicky set out the various toppings and mixes, I was pleased to see that Lou seemed to have loosened up again. She was acting more normally, although I had to admit she was dressed in the style of Jenny Prezzioso, a four-year-old baby-sitting charge of ours who earned the nickname "Miss Priss" when she went through a stage of wearing only lace socks, hair ribbons, and perfectly ironed dresses — and who still can be pretty fussy. Lou was standing on a stool next to the microwave, swathed in an enormous apron over her neat green corduroys and blue-and-green-striped sweater. She was also wearing blue socks and a green headband. Very matching, very perfect. The only things that clashed were the enormous purple oven mitts on her hands.

"It's not popping as much!" she cried.

"Bowls!" cried Mal, passing large bowls down the assembly line (Nicky and the triplets), who lined them up on the table.

When Lou cried, "It's ready, it's ready!" Kristy opened the door and handed her the bag of popcorn. She carried it solemnly to Mal, who opened it carefully (to avoid the initial blast of hot steam) and dumped the popcorn into a bowl.

Then Lou went back to her post, took out a new bag of popcorn, and stuck it into the microwave. With Kristy's help, she punched the numbers to start the oven.

"Thank you, Chef Lou."

Lou giggled. "You're welcome, Chef Kristy."

Maybe Lou had just needed time to get used to the idea of moving, I thought. When her aunt dropped her off, she had been even more reserved than usual. She kept thanking us for inviting her. She glanced at her aunt constantly, as if to make sure she wasn't saying anything wrong.

Luckily, as the afternoon progressed, she definitely become less robotically polite.

I wanted to tell her to calm down and act like a kid.

What bothered me was this: Lou's behavior didn't seem so much polite as careful, as if she were afraid of making a mistake. Lou was having a tough time being a new kid, I figured, and didn't want to take any chances. Maybe she was even worried that her history of extreme misbehavior would be held against her.

Poor Lou. She seemed so young when her aunt had dropped her off — even younger than eight. And yet her face, composed and watchful, had the wary expression of a much older child.

I smiled now at Lou, who was eating double handfuls of popcorn. She smiled back, the first spontaneous smile I think I had seen since she'd returned to Stoneybrook. It made her into a different kid, one I immediately liked better than the hypercareful Louisa McNally.

Although Lou *was* very polite and helpful during the rest of the meeting, she didn't seem so determinedly eager to please. And that, I couldn't help but notice, significantly lowered the disaster factor.

Which is something I brought up at the BSC meeting that afternoon. (Okay, okay. I also brought it up because I could tell by the look in Kristy's eyes that she wanted to talk about my project.)

"You're right," said Stacey. "This is a whole new Lou. It's like she's competing for the Most Unnaturally Polite Kid on the Planet Award."

"Not that there's anything wrong with that," Jessi reminded us.

"No, I'm not saying there is," I explained. I took a handful of garlic nugget pretzels from the bag Claudia was passing around. "But the key word here is 'unnatural.' I appreciate polite, well-behaved kids as much as the next baby-sitter. But it's like Lou is, well, worried all the time. Like, if she isn't absolutely polite, she's going to do something terribly wrong."

"Maybe it's a phase she's going through. That's what my parents always say about my Nancy Drew books," Claudia said.

"Maybe. But why?"

"Because she's new in town and she's got a rep to live down," said Mal. Then she laughed. "Vanessa should hear me — I made a rhyme."

"You're probably right," I said. But I wasn't entirely convinced. Lou was acting like a nervous rabbit — a polite rabbit but a nervous one. What did she have to be afraid of now? She had a caring family, a cool dog, a room of her own, love, attention, even friends — if she'd let herself relax enough to *be* friends with the other kids. It had been clear to me at the last Railroad Project meeting that Hannie was trying her best to be friends with Lou. But she wasn't finding it easy going.

I sighed.

"Are you sighing because of your project?" Kristy asked.

Good old unsubtle Kristy. I hadn't taken her mind off the one subject I wanted to avoid, after all.

"No," I replied.

"How's it going?" Claudia inquired.

"Fine," I said.

Kristy raised her eyebrows. "Really?"

"Really. Why wouldn't it be?" I gave Kristy a hard look. Kristy gave me one back.

"This is going to be a project that Stoneybrook will never forget," I insisted. "I'm thinking of . . . of building a mini replica of a secret passage. Maybe I'll even make a short film about the Underground Railroad. Plus, just to make sure that it *is* a world-class project, I'll publish a guide to the Underground Railroad stops in Stoneybrook. Mary Anne's house wasn't the only one, you know."

"That's true," Mary Anne agreed. "But you better check to make sure that the Stoneybrook Historical Society doesn't already have some kind of guide."

"Even if it does, mine will be better." (Eek. I *had* better check and see what the historical society had. I'd only been there once, about an hour before closing time. I hadn't had time to go through their archives. Mostly I'd just confirmed a lot of the information that I had already dug up at the library.)

"Those are all pretty good ideas," Kristy said.

"Pretty good? Pretty good? What do you mean? They're great," I shot back.

"But you'd better make up your mind, and quick," Madame President added relentlessly.

"Thanks for the input," I snapped.

The phone rang.

"It's for you," I said, and slumped back against the bed in relief.

Kristy was right, not that I'd ever let her know it. I had to come up with a plan. And fast.

CHAPTER 9

Thursday

I'm not crazy about changes, but some of them are good ones. Like getting my father to change his mind about letting me choose my own clothes. And moving to Burnt Hill Road when Dad and Sharon got married. Big changes, but good ones. Well, I guess when you're just a kid, change is extra hard to take. And moving is a big change. For Jay and Lou. And for Carrie and Sean, as I found out....

Boxes, boxes everywhere, and still the Addisons were only half packed. Mary Anne followed Mr. Addison through a house barricaded with boxes. Some of the boxes had labels: DISHES. FRAGILE! ATTIC. VERY FRAGILE!!!! MISC. and more.

"It's a mess," said Mr. Addison, "but we're making progress. Sean! Corrie! Mary Anne is here!"

Mary Anne noticed Mr. Addison was careful not to say, "The baby-sitter is here." Even though Sean was no longer teased by a bully at school for having a baby-sitter, she suspected it was a sensitive subject.

The doorbell rang and Mr. Addison said, "The kids are in the den. That's probably the Nichollses at the door. They're the family who's moving in. They're here to take another look. I'm sure they'll be gone by the time Mrs. Addison and I leave for dinner."

He hurried away and Mary Anne picked her way through the maze of boxes into the den. Sean was watching TV, restlessly channel surfing. Corrie was working on an art project involving what looked like various packing materials.

"Hi, guys," Mary Anne said. "How is everything going?"

"Hi, Mary Anne," Corrie replied cheerfully.

Sean just glanced at Mary Anne, then turned his attention back to the TV.

"I'm in charge of dinner tonight. We're going to make pizza." (Mrs. Addison had called earlier and said that they could send out for pizza. Mary Anne had suggested they make it instead. She thought it might be more fun. Little did she know . . .)

"Pizza! I love pizza," said Corrie.

"Pizza would be okay," said Sean, still watching the channels flick by.

"Why don't we head out to the kitchen and see what we've got in the way of toppings?" Mary Anne suggested.

Corrie immediately began to gather up her art supplies. Sean reluctantly turned off the television.

"Sean, Corrie, I don't believe you've met the Nichollses yet," Mr. Addison said from the doorway.

Mary Anne looked up to see a family of four standing with Mr. Addison: a short man with close-cropped sandy brown hair, a bird-like woman with chin-length blonde hair, and two boys, about five and seven years old. "This is Sean and Corrie, and Mary Anne Spier. If you need a baby-sitter, her baby-sitting club is the one you'll want to call," said Mr. Addison.

"Hello," Mary Anne said. She looked at the two boys. "What're your names?"

"That's Nate," said Mr. Nicholls, indicating the smaller boy, who had big brown eyes and his father's sandy brown hair. "And that's Joey." Joey had his mother's green eyes and dark brown hair. "Nate, Joey, say hello."

"Hello," they both said, almost shyly.

"Hi, Nate. Hi, Joey," Mary Anne replied. "Welcome to Stoneybrook. Where are you moving from?"

"We're from New Jersey," said Mr. Nicholls. He looked at his watch. "I know you're on your way out the door, so let's make this quick."

"Joey and Nate, why don't you come with Sean and Corrie and me to the kitchen and we can get something to drink while your parents look at the house again," Mary Anne offered.

The two boys glanced at their father. "Say thank you," he ordered.

"Thank you," they said in unison, and Mary Anne led the four kids into the kitchen.

Mary Anne got out glasses and poured Apple & Eve Cranberry Raspberry juice. The kitchen was not quite as jammed with boxes as the rest of the house. The Addisons appeared to be saving that job for last. Mary Anne was also relieved to see that most of the cooking utensils were still around.

The kids sat down at the table.

"Aren't you going to have any, Mary Anne?" asked Corrie.

"Not right now," Mary Anne said, checking the refrigerator for the pizza dough.

"We're moving to Seattle," Sean announced.

Nate nodded.

Joey said, "I know where that is, but you don't, Nate."

"I might know," argued Nate.

"You don't," Joey proclaimed, with all the superiority of an older brother. "I do because I'm older."

"Well, I might have known," said Nate.

Mary Anne hid a smile as she found a jar of pizza sauce and put it on the counter.

Mr. and Mrs. Nicholls came into the kitchen, followed by both of the Addisons.

"I think you'll enjoy living here," Mrs. Addison said, looking at Mrs. Nicholls.

Mr. Nicholls rapped out, "Joey, what have I told you about putting your drinking glass directly on a table?"

Mary Anne saw that Nate had put his glass of juice on a folded napkin, but Joey's was sitting on the table. Since the table was basically waterproof, it was not a big deal.

"I'm sorry," Joey said, his voice a sudden squeak.

"It's fine, Mr. Nicholls," Mary Anne said. She

grabbed a towel and wiped up the ring the glass had left. "See?"

Both boys had jumped to their feet. Mr. Nicholls glanced at Mary Anne, then gave Joey a stern look. Mary Anne thought for a second that Joey was going to cry.

Mrs. Nicholls put her hand on her husband's arm, but he shook it off.

Then Mr. Addison said, "No harm done. That's why we have your basic spill-proof kitchen table."

Mary Anne wondered why Mr. Nicholls was so worried about making a good impression. Hadn't he already bought the house?

Mr. Nicholls finally nodded. "Come on, boys."

Joey and Nate practically ran out of the kitchen after their father and mother. *Oh, well*, Mary Anne thought.

After the Addisons and the Nichollses had left, Mary Anne put the pizza dough on the counter. "Corrie, will you find the pizza pan for me?" she asked. "Sean, you're in charge of locating an onion, a green pepper, and whatever else you want on your pizza."

Sean took another sip of juice, looking at Mary Anne levelly over the top of the glass.

"We have a pizza cutter too," said Corrie. "You want that?"

"Yup." Mary Anne rummaged in the cabinets and said, "Do you think your folks would mind if we used this can of artichoke hearts on the pizza?"

Corrie made a face.

"They wouldn't mind, but you would," Mary Anne interpreted. Corrie nodded.

"What about you, Sean? Any food you hate on pizza? Artichokes? Squid?" Mary Anne turned around. Sean hadn't moved, except to fold his arms. He was practically glaring at her.

Mary Anne had been the first BSC member to baby-sit for Sean, and Sean had been so difficult that for a long time Mary Anne had avoided baby-sitting for him again. But she thought, as we all did, that things had smoothed out.

Apparently they hadn't. Trying to keep things light, Mary Anne said, "No artichokes for you either, huh? Okay."

Corrie said, "I'll grate the mozzarella cheese for the topping."

"Great," Mary Anne said. She opened the sauce. Corrie grated the cheese. They worked companionably side by side. When Corrie had finished the mozzarella, she asked if she should turn on the oven.

"Good idea." Mary Anne got out the onion and green pepper (Sean still hadn't moved or spoken) and began to dice the pepper. She glanced over her shoulder and said, "You know, Sean, I bet this pizza would taste even better if you helped make it."

Sean burst out, "You *hate* me, don't you? *Don't you?*"

"What?"

"You heard me," Sean shot back. His face was very red and his lower lip was poking out. He was trying to appear tough, but he still seemed very young.

Carefully putting the knife down, Mary Anne said, "Sean, I don't hate you. Whatever gave you that idea?"

Corrie said, "If anybody hates you, Sean, it's your own fault. You're so *mean* to people."

"Who asked you, cat litter lips?" Sean lashed out.

Before Corrie could retaliate, Mary Anne patted her shoulder. "Corrie, will you give me a few minutes to talk to Sean alone?"

"Have tons of fun," said Corrie, giving Sean a furious look. She stomped out of the kitchen.

Mary Anne sighed. Sean had always been a problem for the BSC, no question about it. They had talked about him more than once, and he had more than his fair share of notes in the BSC notebook.

But no one hated Sean. How could he think that?

"Sean," Mary Anne began gently, "I don't hate you. No one in the Baby-sitters Club hates you. We might have had problems, but people have problems all the time. Even best friends have problems. That doesn't mean they hate each other."

Sean's expression remained stormy. He said, "You're glad to see me go. You're sad to see Corrie go, but you're glad I'm leaving."

"That's not true!"

"What do you think I am, stupid?" Sean jumped up and bolted from the kitchen.

Mary Anne stood there for a moment, shocked to the soles of her feet. She didn't know what to do next. She remembered that one of the reasons Sean was so difficult was because he demanded so much more attention than anyone might expect from a boy his age. He acted out. He took things harder, believed the extreme interpretation of situations. He didn't always see the logical, simple truth.

Mary Anne walked to the kitchen door. "Corrie, Sean, let's finish making this pizza."

Corrie returned immediately. Mary Anne could tell she was curious about what had happened but didn't say anything.

They made pizza. When it was ready, Mary Anne called Sean. He didn't appear. For one awful moment, she thought he'd run out of the house. But she found him sprawled in a chair in the den, his chin on his chest, his hand clutching the television remote.

"Sean," she said. "Pizza's ready."

He shrugged.

"Come on, Sean. Please?"

At last he got up. He brushed past her into the kitchen. Corrie chatted cheerfully as they ate dinner. Sean didn't say a word, no matter how much Mary Anne tried to reach him. By the time she left, she was exhausted and felt very sorry for Sean.

She hated the idea of him leaving Stoneybrook thinking that no one in the BSC could stand him. But what could we do? The going-away party we'd been planning to throw for Corrie and Sean somehow didn't seem to be enough.

Maybe nothing we could do would change the way Sean felt.

CHAPTER 10

When Mary Anne told me about Sean, I was genuinely surprised — and bothered. But I didn't have time to think about it much. I had to focus on my barely existent project, or else.

I'd taken videos of some of the kids inside the secret passage in Mary Anne's house. They had measured it and talked about how it would have felt to be a fugitive slave hiding there. We'd had another meeting of the Railroad Project. I'd videotaped that. I'd done more research, both at the library and at the Stoneybrook Historical Society.

I had a ton of material. And nothing to turn in.

I made another trek to the historical society after school on Friday. As I was sitting in one of the two rooms that housed the society's archives, Ms. Kellogg, who is president of the society, said, "You might find it interesting to look at the originals of some of our materials. You will have to be very careful with them, of course. Some of this documentation is two hundred years old."

A little while later, she returned, holding several papers, each of them individually sealed in protective plastic covers. Some of the papers were letters. One, of which Ms. Kellogg was very proud, was an actual wanted poster for Harriet Tubman. "This is quite rare and valuable," she explained to me. "Harriet Tubman often hired sympathizers and fellow Railroad members to follow the people who put these posters up. They would take them down and destroy them almost as soon as they went up."

I nodded, staring in awe at the yellowed wanted poster, trying to imagine the courage of Harriet Tubman.

"And here," said Ms. Kellogg, "are a few newspapers from that time. We have a complete archive of newspapers reaching back throughout Stoneybrook's history, thanks to the generosity of donors."

"Thanks," I said. I had looked at lots of newspaper articles on the microfiche machine at the library, but none of them had the impact of seeing the actual newspapers of the time, of seeing the stories about running-aways (as the slaves running to freedom were called) juxtaposed against the stories of weather and crops, births and deaths, elections and laws.

The articles were long and wordy and full of opinions, not at all like modern journalism, which (as we'd learned in school) isn't necessarily objective, even when it appears to be.

And then it hit me: My project would be a news report. I would take the story of a fugitive and make it into a sort of documentary television report, formatted like the television show *60 Minutes*.

I put the newspapers down carefully, jumped up, and did a little victory dance, right there in the Stoneybrook Historical Society. Then I sat down and got to work. After all, I had a news story to turn in, and I was on a deadline.

"Thank you all for coming," I said. I looked at the faces of the members of the Railroad Project. Everyone looked back at me. No one spoke. I sensed that the original enthusiasm of the group had waned, thanks in part to my inability to decide exactly what my project would entail.

"I've decided what my project is going to be," I went on.

More silence.

I saw Kristy raise her eyebrows and silently willed her to speak up. But she didn't.

Then good old Mal chimed in, "What? Tell us, Abby."

I gave Mal a warm smile. I said, "We're going to do a *60 Minutes*–style news report on a fugitive who has made it as far as Stoneybrook, Connecticut. We'll use some of the stories from our research on the Underground Railroad and create a fictional character to report on. We'll interview abolitionists, have anonymous interviews with conductors, speak to a Quaker, a free man or woman, and all the other people who might be involved."

There was another silence, but this time it wasn't disinterested. I could practically hear people thinking. Then Vanessa said, "Can I be Dinah Sawyer? Or an abolitionist lawyer?"

My eyes met Mal's and then Kristy's. We cracked up. It was a very good feeling.

"We're standing in front of the home of Abigail Grey, a Quaker and well-known member of the abolitionist movement here in the little town of Stoneybrook, Connecticut." Vanessa was dressed (she said) like a "television journalist," with her hair pulled back and a pair of her mother's old glasses (minus the lenses) on her nose. She turned to interview "Abigail."

There really was a Quaker abolitionist named Abigail Grey who had lived in Stoneybrook. Her house is now on the Stoneybrook

Historical Society register of historic places. Of course, we'd gotten permission from the current owners before we shot the scene.

"Abigail" (played by Hannie Papadakis) was dressed in an approximation of Quaker clothing from the time. We'd borrowed some clothes from the costume department at Stoneybrook High School and Claudia had led an independent clothes-making session involving even more baby-sitting charges, which I had videotaped, naturally. I had also videotaped the session during which we had gathered around to write the newscast and choose who was going to do what.

I had gotten some fairly spectacular and unplanned footage of Lou in her super-polite and helpful mode. She'd tried running the sewing machine at Mary Anne's, and in addition to sewing several pieces of different costumes together had almost stitched her finger into the machine. I don't know who screamed louder — Lou or Claudia.

This will be cut from the final version.

Then Lou had tried to help print the draft of the story that I had written up on my computer. She'd hit the wrong button and erased quite a bit of material.

I only screamed silently. "Don't worry, Lou," I told her. "Happens all the time."

I stayed up until one A.M. rewriting the story.

86

After that, I tried to give Lou assignments that wouldn't endanger me, her, or anyone else. What I wanted to do, more than anything, was to tell Lou to relax and take it easy. Talk to Hannie, I wanted to say. Hang out with Karen Brewer (who had also joined the project) and with Becca. Although most of the kids were involved in Black History Month projects with their own classes, word had spread that this was going to be cool. My project had become a kid magnet, and I had more volunteers than I knew what to do with.

So I wrote a scene into the script that showed a mob of angry people facing down a posse of slave hunters outside Mary Anne's house. Now everyone had a role.

This would have been a perfect opportunity for Lou to make friends, as Jay was doing. He'd lost a lot of his solemn caution during our rehearsals, and he and Linny seemed to be on their way to best friendship, boy-style. (They made lots of gross noises with their noses and punched each other's arms at every opportunity.)

But Lou, although she seemed to enjoy Hannie's company, rarely left my side, volunteering for everything and trying way, way too hard. I liked Lou, but she was beginning to wear me out.

I wondered if anyone else had noticed, her

brother perhaps. Maybe, I thought, I could have a word with him and he could have a word with Lou without hurting her feelings.

So during a filming break (and after I sent Lou to help Claudia and some of the other kids bring hot cider to the crew), I called Jay over for a conference.

We sat on a couple of bales of hay inside the barn. "How's everything going?" I asked.

Jay looked me over, as if he suspected I was asking a trick question. Then he smiled and said, "This is great. We never got to do projects like this at our old school."

"Good. I guess Lou is having fun too?"

"Sure."

Jay wasn't giving anything away.

"I wondered about Lou, because she, well, she's working so hard to help out that she, ah, well, doesn't seem to have much time to enjoy being part of the project."

After regarding me for a long moment, Jay said, "Lou's trying really hard to be good. It's sort of weird, I guess."

I said quickly, "I'm glad Lou wants to help. But sometimes she seems to be overdoing it."

There. I'd said it. I waited.

"I know," Jay replied, looking down at his hands. He went on. "Lou wasn't always like this." He flashed a smile. "Ask anyone."

I nodded.

"I mean, this isn't the real Lou. My sister's nice, but she's not a fake nice kid or anything. It's just that she wants to belong to a family."

"She *does*," I blurted out.

"I know. I know Aunt Sarabeth and Uncle Mac adopted us, and all. But what if that went wrong? What if they . . . died? Or had to give us up? I mean, I know it probably won't happen, but it did happen to us once already, when our mother left us with Dad and then Dad, you know, died."

"Oh, Jay," I said, remembering vividly my own father's dying.

And then I thought of something that I, amazingly, had never thought about before. What if something happened to Mom too? What would happen to Anna and me?

It made my stomach hurt to think about it. I sniffed.

Jay looked up at me. "Are you okay?" he asked.

"Hay," I said quickly. "Allergies."

"Oh." He smiled a little. "Anyway, Lou's trying to be perfect, I guess. That way, no one will ever have any reason not to want her again."

At that moment, Karen came running into the barn with Hannie. "I want to ride in the box," she said.

One of the scenes in my documentary, taken

from a true story, was going to show several boxes being loaded onto a wagon in front of the house. We were going to use the wagon from Mary Anne's barn. (If we angled the camera just right, no one would ever know that there weren't any horses attached to it.) Later, it would be revealed that the fugitive had been in one of the boxes and had escaped right under the posse's nose.

"Thanks, Jay," I said, knowing that Karen and Hannie had effectively put an end to our conversation.

"Sure," he responded, jumping up. "I'm going to get some cider. Would you like some?"

"In a minute, thanks." Jay had given me a lot to think about. Unfortunately, I didn't have time to do so at the moment.

"*No one* is riding in any of the boxes," I told Karen and Hannie, who had begun to climb aboard.

"Why not?" Karen asked.

"Because it would make it too heavy for one person to lift. We'd have to hire Arnold Schwarzenegger, and he's not in the budget."

This headed off the argument, and we went back to work. I only had one more day after this to finish shooting. Then I'd have three days to pull the project together.

We hauled the wagon out of the barn for the

box scene. It was hard work. That old wagon was heavy!

Lou was right there the whole time, pushing, pulling, and panting. Then she offered to get me a glass of water. When I didn't want water, she offered cider. "I don't have time right now," I told her. "It'll be too dark to video soon."

Lou apologized for not realizing that and then vanished. As Vanessa "Sawyer," Nicky (the head of the posse), and Byron (the owner of the house) went nose to nose, Karen, Hannie, and Adam began to bring boxes out of the house and load them onto the wagon.

At that moment, Lou trotted out the front door with a thermos and headed toward me.

"Here," she said. "I put some hot cider in the thermos so you can drink it when you have time."

She ruined the shot.

I turned off the camera and said, "CUT!" To Lou I said, "Lou, you just walked right into the middle of a scene."

Lou looked around and then said, "Oh, I'm sorry. I didn't mean to. Is it ruined forever?"

I looked up at the sky. "I think we've got time to shoot it once more. Everybody, back to your places. And hurry!"

Everybody hurried. Lou said, "Are you mad,

Abby? Please don't be mad at me. You won't tell my aunt and uncle, will you? I'm really, really sorry."

I was staring through the camera, trying to concentrate. But it was hard. I lowered the camera once more. "Lou," I said. "Will you lighten up, for Pete's sake? It's no big deal. So quit making it into one."

Lou's eyes widened. "I'm . . . I'm sorry," she stammered.

"And don't apologize. You don't need to. You've done enough of that already."

I'd meant to be kinder and gentler when I said that, and much more tactful and understanding. As you can see, I wasn't.

Lou took a step back. "I'm sorry," she said again. "I mean, it won't happen again." She kept backing up as she spoke, as if she wanted to put a safe distance between us.

"We're ready!" Karen called from just inside the front door of the house.

I wanted to call Lou back. But there wasn't time.

With a heavy heart I raised the camera. "Action!" I called.

CHAPTER 11

The weather held for the last day of the shoot. I'd spent the whole night working on my project. The more I worked, the more I could see what needed to be done.

I was going to try to get in a few key scenes that afternoon, including the big finale, in which the crowd fends off the posse, giving the fugitive in the box time to escape. We'd even included a harrowing moment when the leader, Nicky, demands that the wagon be searched to make sure it doesn't have a false bottom.

We got to work. At first, things went smoothly. Mal had returned with Vanessa and her brothers. Kristy had come too, along with Claudia. We had a good ratio of baby-sitters to kids, which proved to be an excellent thing.

Why? Because Lou had decided she no longer had to be the Best Kid Ever.

At first, when the actors kept giggling and

goofing around, I thought it was because they were tired of all the work. "Just a little while longer," I said.

The giggling continued. "The more you goof off, the longer we'll be here," Kristy announced in her drill-sergeant voice. That helped, but only for a little while.

The cameras rolled. "Check the wagon," Nicky (in character) cried. "Make sure it doesn't have a false bottom. I'm wise to the tricks of these lawbreakers!"

Everyone turned toward the wagon. Karen stood there, holding a box, looking suspiciously innocent.

Hannie (as Abigail) said indignantly, "We break no laws of any civilized country."

"Step aside," Nicky roared.

Suddenly, the box on the wagon popped open and Lou jumped up. "Surprise!" she said, and burst out laughing.

All the other kids laughed too.

I lowered the camera in shock. "Lou," I said. "What are you doing?"

Lou kept bowing to her audience, ignoring me. Claudia stepped up to the wagon, caught Lou under each arm, and lifted her down.

"Good one, Lou," said Adam.

Even Jay was smiling.

"Lou," I said, "I don't have much time here. So don't do that again, okay?"

"Okay," Lou said carelessly, and scooted back into the crowd.

I kept a close eye on Lou after that, at least for awhile. Then I became so involved in the project that I forgot about her.

Even then, I didn't associate all the little things that kept going wrong with Lou. After all, she was no longer right under my feet, trying to help out (and getting in the way).

I didn't think of Lou when I looked through the camera in Dawn's room (which we'd tried to make look as much as possible like a room from the Underground Railroad era) and noticed that mustaches had been drawn on all the pictures we had hung on the wall. (We'd copied sepia photographs from the library and put them in borrowed picture frames.)

Fortunately, the mustaches wiped easily off the glass.

"Who did this?" I asked.

Everyone turned and looked at Lou. She grinned.

"Lou, cut it out," I said.

"It was funny," Lou said. "Besides, you told me to lighten up."

Before I could continue, four of the kids blew huge bubble-gum bubbles in Nicky's face and made him start laughing.

Where had they gotten the gum?

"Lou," I said, without even asking.

"It was just for fun," Lou said. She looked at me from under her eyelashes. "Lighten up, Abby."

Great. I'd created a monster. I shot Kristy a Look that said, "Help me."

"Why don't you come stand over here with me, Lou?" Kristy suggested.

That worked until Kristy was distracted by an argument between Linny and Jordan. I was videotaping the "posse" as they walked around the house, "searching" each room.

Nicky and Hannie opened a closet door, and Lou jumped out, screaming "BOO!" at the top of her lungs.

It's one of the oldest, dumbest tricks in the book. I guess that's why it works every time.

We all jumped and screamed. I jumped the highest and dropped the camera.

I watched it fall in super-slow motion, a sick feeling in the pit of my stomach.

It landed on my toe. I shouted "Ouch," but at the same time I instinctively flipped my foot up. The camera rose in the air again — and Jay caught it.

We all stood there, frozen. Then Kristy said, "Nice move, Jay, Abby."

I thanked Jay in a faint voice. "I owe you one, big-time."

Jay smiled. "Cool."

Linny punched Jay's arm. Jay punched Linny's arm.

For one moment, Lou looked almost sorry. Then her chin went up.

Mine did too, and I think I must have looked like I was about to lose it. Claudia stepped in, grabbed Lou by the hand, and said, "Come on, Lou. Let's start putting things back in their places."

Before Lou could protest, Stacey had swept her out of the room and out of certain danger. As Lou left, she looked over my shoulder and gave me a sweet, wicked smile. "Lighten up, Abby," she said again.

That's when I realized that I had to have a talk with Lou — before she once again became the Worst Kid Ever.

Tuesday

When you were at the Addisons,
Mary Anne, it was box city. When I
got there, they'd made lots of progress.
And I think we made some progress
with Sean too, with Operation We Don't
Hate Sean... at least until I made that
one little mistake.

When Stacey arrived at the Addisons', many of the boxes had been filled, taped, labeled, and moved to the dining room.

Mr. and Mrs. Addison welcomed Stacey warmly but seemed surprised to see Mary Anne and Jessi as well. "We just wanted to say good-bye and good luck," Stacey explained.

"Thanks," said Mrs. Addison. "I know Corrie and Sean are going to miss you all."

Maybe, thought Stacey. *Maybe not*.

"We're going to the bank to close our accounts," explained Mr. Addison, "and to run a few errands. We shouldn't be gone long."

"No problem," Stacey assured him.

Stacey, Mary Anne, and Jessi found Sean and Corrie in the den. But Sean wasn't watching television. He was actually sprawled on the floor next to Corrie, trying his hand at an art project.

That was because the television had been boxed, as had almost everything else in the den except the chairs, a lamp, and the rug.

Sean looked up and scowled. "What are you doing here?"

"Well, we had a special game we wanted to play, and it takes more than one friend to play it."

Stacey half expected Sean to say *You're not*

99

my friends, but he didn't. He kept scowling, although he looked sort of interested.

"What's the game?" Corrie asked.

"It's a Sean game," said Jessi. "Stacey, Mary Anne, and I have taken a vote and elected you King of the Hour."

"Yeah? So?" The scowl had almost disappeared.

Corrie looked up warily. "What does that mean?"

"It means that Sean gets to be king for an hour. He can do anything he wants to, within reason. We're his loyal and obedient subjects," Jessi explained.

"I don't know about that," said Corrie.

Mary Anne said, "Don't worry, Corrie. It'll be fun."

Meanwhile, the game had definitely gotten Sean's attention. "King," he said. "King Sean." He clearly liked the sound of that. Then he looked at Stacey. "Anything?"

"Within reason," Stacey repeated.

"I want to go sledding at the SMS hill," Sean said. "And every time I sled to the bottom, someone has to pull me back up to the top. *And* give me a push."

"You've got it," said Stacey.

Everyone bundled up. After Stacey had left a note for Sean's parents, they all walked to SMS. The hill is a good-sized one at the foot of the school yard. The snow had been packed down hard by millions of sleds. A few kids were sledding there when Sean and his loyal royal subjects arrived.

He waved at a thickset blond boy and said, "Hey, Mel!"

The boy glanced at Sean, then waved back, a little reluctantly, it seemed. Stacey smiled. Mel was the bully who had once teased Sean about having a baby-sitter until Sean, with Stacey's help, had found a way to stop him.

Satisfied that he had Mel's attention, Sean sat down on his sled and said, "Okay. Pull me to the top."

Stacey and Jessi grabbed the sled and began to haul Sean up the hill. Mary Anne helped Corrie pull her sled up.

At the top of the hill, they gave Sean a big push. He shot down, screaming loudly as the sled swooshed far out into the school yard. When he reached the bottom, he stood up. "Come on," he said. "I want to go again."

Mary Anne and Stacey pulled Sean up the hill. He sailed down again. Stacey went down to help. Then Jessi. Then Mary Anne again.

Sean waved at other kids and shouted greetings each time he was pulled to the top. Sometimes he called to whoever was pulling him, "Faster, faster!"

"Yes, King Sean," Stacey (or Jessi or Mary Anne) would say, and pull a little harder.

Sean had a great time. In fact, he was having such a great time that they let him be king for almost an hour and a half. But at last Stacey looked at her watch and said, "Okay, King Sean. This is the last ride."

He was given one more push off the hill. Then the BSC gave Corrie a push and followed her down.

"That was *great*," Sean cried as they walked home. "Did you see how far I went? And super-fast. You guys give good push-offs."

"Thanks," said Jessi a bit breathlessly.

"I like being king. You should try it, Corrie."

"I'd like to," said Corrie.

The Addisons' car pulled into the driveway as they turned the corner near the house. At just about the same time, Stacey got her breath back. "Whew," she said. "That was hard work. I'm glad it's over."

Wrong thing to say.

Sean stopped in his tracks, his eyebrows drawing together in a thunderous frown. "What?"

"It was hard work pulling you up that hill," said Stacey, sensing only dimly that she'd said something to upset Sean.

"You're glad it's over!" said Sean. "That's what you said. You didn't even want to play

King of the Hour. You're glad I'm moving. I knew it. *I knew it!*"

"Sean, wait," said Stacey, but it was too late.

Sean grabbed his sled out of Stacey's hand and ran to the house. They heard the crash of the sled as he threw it into the garage.

Sean ran inside, past his parents.

"Hey," called Mr. Addison. "Sledding? Good idea. I don't think we're going to see a lot of snow in Seattle."

"Have fun?" asked Mrs. Addison.

"I did," said Corrie.

"Sledding is always fun," said Mary Anne diplomatically.

But no one was sure what Sean's answer would have been. Maybe Sean would realize that the BSC didn't hate him. Or maybe one innocent statement had made things worse than ever.

CHAPTER 13

I'd been working on my project nonstop, and thinking about Lou.

This was, perhaps, natural, since I was supposed to baby-sit for Lou and Jay that afternoon while their aunt and uncle were at a meeting.

But, of course, that wasn't the only reason. As I walked up the steps to the McNallys' house, I realized that I didn't know which Lou I was going to meet on the other side of that front door — the Worst Kid Ever, or the Best.

If the way a kid is dressed is a tip-off, then Lou's clothing proclaimed that she had reclaimed her Best Kid role. She met me at the door in her corduroy pants, a long-sleeved rugby shirt, matching socks, and a coordinating headband. It was nice and neat, and not Lou's style at all.

"Hey, Lou, how's it going?" I asked.

"Fine, thank you," said Lou. "How are you? How is your project?"

"Fine, and fine. In fact, I think my project might be the best project in the history of the world."

Lou smiled. Politely. Then she said, "I'm sorry if I was not, you know, well-behaved the other day." She looked over her shoulder as if she was afraid someone might overhear her. Then she went on. "I was only kidding. You don't, you know, need to tell anybody, do you?"

"What's to tell?" I said. "No problem."

"Hi, Abby," said Mrs. McNally, who was followed by Jay and by Happy, who was apparently being propelled by her wildly wagging tail.

"Hey, Happy," I said.

"These guys have to do their homework first. Then they have free time. We'll be home in time for dinner," Mrs. McNally told me as she took her coat out of the hall closet. "Mac's already at the meeting. We won't be long."

"Did you leave a phone number where I can reach you, just in case?" I asked.

"In case of what?" Lou asked.

"Standard baby-sitters' procedure," I explained. "It's a Baby-sitters Club rule."

"And a good one," Lou's aunt agreed. "The

number is by the phone in the kitchen." She smiled at Lou and me. "Be good and have fun," she said.

"I'll be good," Lou answered solemnly. She reached up and hugged her aunt. I watched as Mrs. McNally gently unwrapped Lou's stranglehold. "I know you will, Lou," she said, and kissed Lou on the cheek.

Lou watched until her aunt was out the door. Then she turned to me. Her tense body seemed to relax a fraction.

"I guess I should go finish my homework," Jay grumbled.

"Or we could play a game," Lou suggested.

"Homework first, games second," I said.

"Okay." Lou sighed. "I don't have much anyway. I have to draw a picture of the food pyramid. You know, all the healthy food you're supposed to eat every day."

Jay said teasingly, "Is your teacher going to let you count chocolate chip cookies as one of the food groups?"

"She should," Lou answered, grinning at her brother. "Come on, Happy."

After Jay and Lou were safely working, I settled down on the sofa to catch up on some of the homework I'd been neglecting because of my project. I knocked off a few math problems and raised my head to do the baby-sitter radar scan. The house was very quiet. Was it too quiet?

I stood up and went to Jay's room.

"I'm almost done," he announced. He was sitting at his desk, his homework spread out in front of him.

I found Lou on the floor of her room, a large poster in front of her. Happy was sprawled out on the bed, watching Lou intently.

Lou had filled in the food pyramid. Then she'd made a list down one side that said, "More Food Groups." Sure enough, chocolate chip cookies were at the top of the list.

"Lou, you are too much," I said.

She smiled at me and jumped up. "All I have to do is sign it," she said. She selected a red pen, squatted down, and wrote in big, blocky letters LOU WAS HERE. "Now let's set the table for dinner," she suggested. "We can surprise Aunt Sarabeth and Uncle Mac."

"Good idea," I agreed.

Jay liked the idea too, as long as we could play a game afterward.

"If we have time," I promised.

Lou raced away. Jay and I followed. When we reached the kitchen, I turned on the light (funny — I thought the kitchen light had been on), and Lou leaped out and screamed, "BOO!"

I leaped back and crashed into Jay.

Jay said, "Lou! Are you nuts?"

Lou doubled over with glee. "I gotcha!" she declared.

"Lou, don't do stuff like that. It's not funny."

"*I'm* laughing."

"Lou," I said warningly.

"Oh, okay. I won't do it again. Sorry." But she didn't sound sorry. I decided to accept the apology anyway and went into the kitchen. It was clear to me that Lou could go from Worst to Best and back again at bewildering speed.

We'd just finished setting the table when Lou accidentally dropped a plate. It shattered.

Lou shrieked.

I came running, half expecting it to be one of Lou's jokes. But it wasn't. She was staring down at the shards of broken china with a horrified expression on her face.

"Lou? Are you okay?" I asked.

She looked up at me, ashen-faced. Her lips seemed to move stiffly. She whispered, "I'm sorry."

"I'll get the broom," Jay volunteered cheerfully.

"I'm sorry," Lou repeated.

"It's just a plate, Lou," I said. "Accidents happen."

"I'm sorry, I'm sorry, I'm sorry." Lou could not stop apologizing, her voice rising with each repetition. She ran blindly forward. If I hadn't caught her, she might have run right through the wall. I heard china fragments crunch and was grateful that she was wearing her shoes.

Jay returned as Lou burst into noisy sobs. "I didn't mean to do it!" she cried.

Jay grabbed Happy, who'd come barreling in to investigate the noise. He shoved her into another room while he swept up the china. I led Lou into the den. I sat her down on the sofa next to me, keeping one arm around her. Her small body shook with sobs.

"Lou," I said soothingly, "it's not the end of the world. It's just the end of a plate."

She kept crying. I stroked her hair and patted her back.

Jay came into the den with Happy bounding next to him. "Come on, Lou. It's okay."

"No it's not." She choked out her words and I felt her fists clench around my neck.

Jay put one hand on Lou's shoulder and gave it a little shake. "Why not?" he said.

She raised her tear-streaked face to look at him. "Because they'll give me away. They'll send me back because I'm bad. They won't keep me."

Lou really *did* believe that. How awful, and how heartbreaking.

"Lou, that's just not true," I said.

"No way," Jay agreed, sitting down on the

other side of her. She butted her head against his chest and kept on crying.

"They will," she insisted. "They'll send me to live with another family."

"We went to court," Jay said indignantly. "They couldn't send us to live with another family even if they wanted to. And they don't. Adoption is forever."

Lou's sobs lessened. But she said, "You're good. But I'm not. They could just send me away."

"Aunt Sarabeth and Uncle Mac would never do that. Never. And besides, I wouldn't let them," said Jay.

"You couldn't stop them after Daddy died," Lou argued. "They sent me away without you."

Happy, who had been watching us intently, gave a little yip and leaned up to try to lick Lou's face. Lou smiled a woebegone smile.

Then I heard the front door open. Happy gave another yip and scampered down the hall. A moment later she came back with the McNallys behind her.

"Lou? Jay? What happened?" said Mrs. McNally, taking in the scene at one glance.

I cleared my throat. But Jay beat me to it.

"Lou broke a plate and she thinks you're going to give her — us — back if she's bad."

"Oh, Lou," cried Mrs. McNally. She was

across the room in one stride, her arms around both Lou and Jay. "No! Never. Ever! Not in a thousand years! Mac and I love you and Jay more than *anything*."

I stood up. It was time for me to go. The McNallys didn't need me to work this out.

When I got home, I went into my mother's study and hugged her hard. We're not big on hugs and sentimental, mushy stuff in our family, but Mom gave me one look over the top of the half glasses she wears for reading and then pulled me onto her lap as if I were a little kid.

I didn't protest.

"Hard day?" asked Mom.

"Maybe," I said, remembering Dad. My grip tightened on my mother. "I'm glad you're here," I said.

"I'm glad too," said Mom.

"Yeah," I said, and sighed with happiness — and a little sadness too.

CHAPTER 14

I was tired, I was totally energized. I was calm, I was out of my mind. It was the best of times, it was the worst of times. . . .

Wait a minute. That last line is from *A Tale of Two Cities*, a book by Charles Dickens.

It was project day at the Stoneybrook Community Center. Although it was Saturday, I got up much, much earlier than I usually do, even when I'm planning a long run. I checked to make sure that I had the tape I had made about the Underground Railroad (which I had called *Invisible Tracks to Freedom*). Then I checked to make sure I had my two backup copies.

I looked at the clock. I wanted to call Mal's house. Surely her family would be up this early, even on a Saturday. I mean, everyone knows that large families, especially large families with small children, don't sleep late.

My hand hovered over the telephone, but I pulled it back.

I decided to make myself a cup of hot tea instead.

"Abby?" Anna peered at me sleepily from the door of the kitchen. "Aren't you up awfully early?"

"I have to get to the community center soon to set up my project," I said.

She squinted at the clock on the kitchen wall. "Of course, I can't be sure without my glasses, but that clock seems to say it's seven in the morning, and the center doesn't even open until nine, right?"

"Are you sure that clock is working?" I said, struck by a horrifying thought. "What if it stopped? What if we've already overslept? What if that's why . . ."

Anna walked into the kitchen and picked up my wrist. She raised it and I was face-to-face with my watch. It read 7:01, and as I watched, it flipped over to read 7:02.

"Right," I said sheepishly.

"I'm going back to bed." Anna yawned. "See you in an hour."

At the community center, we were all assigned booths in the enormous, all-purpose common room. The "booths" were empty spaces broken up by rope dividers. Everywhere I looked, people were busily setting up their projects.

"Chairs," I barked to Anna. "Table."

I signed in with the person in charge and raced to the car. Mom and I wrestled a sturdy table into the common room and set it up at the very back of my booth against the wall. That was for the television. Then we brought in chairs and lined them up two by two on either side of a small aisle. At the front of the booth, to one side, we set up a smaller folding table. On it I put my programs and an information sheet. Then I hung up a poster that Claudia had made. It read ALL ABOARD THE UNDERGROUND RAILROAD. Beneath that it read VIDEO DOCUMENTARY BY ABIGAIL STEVENSON. Then it listed the show times.

My tape had ended up being twenty minutes long. That sounds short, doesn't it? But it had taken me hours and hours and hours to put together all the video footage I had made into one cohesive story.

Where was Mal? She was going to help me with crowd control. I looked at my watch. I looked up and down the rows of booths.

I saw the triplets and Mr. Pike. Mal, Nicky, and Vanessa were behind them. I waved my arms and heard Byron say, "There she is!"

"This is cool," said Adam. "Can we look around?"

"Sure," said Mr. Pike. He smiled at me. "All set, Abby?"

"All set, Mr. Pike," I said.

He nodded and smiled, then left with Nicky and Vanessa.

Mal looked around my booth. Compared to some of the hyperactivity at the other booths, mine was an oasis of calm. I was ready.

"Wow," Mallory said. "You must have gotten here at dawn."

I grinned. "Practically."

"Is Anna here?"

"She and Mom went to get some breakfast. I, uh, kind of didn't give them much time for it this morning."

"Intense," commented Mallory. Then she said, "You mind if I look around?"

"Go ahead," I said. "Just be back in time for the grand premiere." I pointed at the sign at the front of the booth. "Seating is limited."

"I'll be here," Mallory promised.

Seating *was* limited. In fact, for the premiere, it was standing room only. I looked out at the crowd of people in my booth and felt an enormous rush of pride. My friends hadn't let me down. Every BSC member was there, plus all the kids who had participated in the documentary, plus their families. Claudia closed the "ticket" box (she'd made free tickets to the Underground Railroad, which she'd handed to each person who walked into the booth, along with a program).

Lou was dressed in her neat, clean Best Kid

Ever clothes . . . without the matching head-band. She "ushered" people to their seats. "I think you'll enjoy our movie," I heard her telling people earnestly.

When everyone was seated and the standing room had been filled, I cleared my throat and held up the program. "Welcome to the pre-miere screening of *Invisible Tracks to Freedom*," I said. "I couldn't have made this video without the help of my friends, and I'd like to thank each and every one of you." With that, I read the list of names in the program. When I had finished, the crowd burst into applause. Lou, who was sitting up front on the floor with Hannie and Karen and some of the other kids, jumped to her feet and took bows. The ap-plause intensified and a ripple of laughter spread through the crowd. The other kids jumped up and joined Lou.

I let them take their bows. They'd earned it. Then, as the applause died down, I held up my hand again. "Thank you. And now, *Invisible Tracks to Freedom*." I pushed the tape into the VCR and pressed PLAY.

The title and the credits appeared on the TV screen. It had taken a lot of work, but I had managed to pair each person's name with a moment of footage showing him or her doing something on the tape.

Then we cut to the planning stages. We listened to different kids talk about what they thought the Underground Railroad was. From there I showed our research and planning. I included shots of sewing sessions and art sessions, fitting sessions and rehearsals.

And then "Vanessa Sawyer" appeared on the screen to announce that it was believed a fugitive was hiding in Stoneybrook, a known stop on the Underground Railroad. Vanessa held up the photocopy of an old Stoneybrook newspaper and read aloud from it. Then she said, "Let's take a closer look at this train, which has conductors, stations, stationmasters, passengers — but no tracks."

I watched the video and the audience. I had seen it so many times as I was working on the tape that I couldn't be sure anymore if it was as good as I thought it was. The editing was choppy and the performances were amateur. But at the end of the tape, I got a standing ovation.

I bowed. Then I said to Lou and all the others, "Come up here and take a bow with me."

Lou leaped to her feet and raced to the front of the crowd.

"Come on, come on," she shouted excitedly at Kristy, Stacey, Claudia, Jessi, Mallory, Mary Anne, Logan, and Shannon.

So the BSC members came to the front too.

The applause lasted for almost a minute.

And as I listened to it and looked around at my friends, I realized that even if I hadn't done the best project in the history of the school, I didn't mind. In spite of all the pressure I'd put on myself — pressure as intense in some ways as the pressure Lou had put on herself — I'd enjoyed working on the project. And I'd learned, all over again, that there was something even more important than doing the best project in the history of the world.

Having friends.

Corny? Yes. True? Yes.

From now on, I resolved, I was going to be a little easier on myself and on other people.

Although it didn't seem possible, I grinned even more widely and took another bow.

CHAPTER 15

The Addisons had waved good-bye to their furniture. The next time they would see it, the movers would be unloading it in their new house in Seattle.

Tonight, they were going to stay with friends. Tomorrow, they would get on a plane to Seattle.

We held the going-away party at Kristy's, since she has the biggest house. (I don't think that's the only reason she volunteered her house. I think she likes having parties there because she can be even more in charge.)

We're not only expert baby-sitters, we're expert party givers too. We had adult food (clam dip, *eccch!*) and kid food (chocolate chip cookies). We had great decorations (thanks to Mallory and Claudia). We had games for the kids to play in the house without tearing it down (Jessi and Stacey were in charge of that), and we had a cleanup committee (all the rest of us).

When the Addisons arrived, I think my friends and I felt a little worried. Would Sean still be angry with us? We didn't know what to expect.

Corrie skipped up the stairs, holding a big roll of white paper. "Claudia!" she cried. "Look! I brought my portrait of Stoneybrook to finish."

Mrs. Addison laughed. "I'm not sure how we're going to carry it on the plane, but she wouldn't let us pack it and send it with the other stuff."

"We can finish it today, and then I'll mail it to you," Claudia told Corrie.

"Can you?" asked Corrie.

"Absolutely. They make special mailing tubes for things like this."

Mr. Addison then introduced us to Mr. and Mrs. Nicholls and their sons, Joey and Nate. He explained that they were moving into the Addisons' house.

I nodded. Mary Anne had mentioned the Nichollses.

"Hello," I said. "I'm glad to meet you."

"Hello," said Mr. Nicholls. "Joey and Nate, say hello to Abby."

"Hello," the boys said in unison. Mrs. Nicholls murmured something indistinct but friendly.

"Go and get some refreshments," Mr. Nicholls commanded.

The boys started in the direction of the refreshment table. Nate bumped someone's elbow.

"Be careful!" Mr. Nicholls barked. "Do you want to make someone spill all over the rug?"

Nate froze.

Stacey approached him and said, "Hi, guys. I'm Stacey. Why don't we get some food and you can meet some of the other kids."

The boys looked at their father. He nodded. "Behave," he ordered.

They nodded and went off with Stacey.

I noticed that Mr. Nicholls watched them like a hawk. And I noticed that the boys glanced often in their father's direction. Sometimes he motioned to them. Sometimes he nodded or shook his head. And sometimes he just gave them a stern look.

Whatever he did, they seemed to obey, like remote-control puppets. Wow. Was he uptight. I hoped he'd loosen up once their move was over.

I drifted away and discovered a knot of kids standing around Claudia and Corrie, who had unrolled the big sheet of paper on the floor of the den. It was clearly a kid magnet. Most of Corrie's friends were standing around, offering suggestions.

Claudia looked at Corrie. "Maybe we should let everybody draw just one thing on your portrait of Stoneybrook. What do you think?"

"I think yes," said Corrie. She looked around. "You all have to draw a self-portrait. *And* sign your name."

Corrie was taking the move well. But what about Sean?

I glanced around. He was standing at the edge of the room, his hands in his pockets.

Mary Anne said, "I think we should go talk to Sean."

"Okay," I said. I snagged a cup of punch and a plate of kid food. "Here. We'll take him this."

We walked toward Sean. I admit, I kept a tight hold on the plate, waiting to see how he was going to react. Sean was capable of flipping the plate right out my hands if he was unhappy or angry enough.

But Sean surprised us. He looked up and his face looked positively woeful.

"Sean?" said Mary Anne. "We brought you some punch and cookies."

He took the punch but said softly, "I'm not very hungry."

"Why not?" I asked.

"Because."

"Because why?"

"Because I don't want to go. I like it here. I

know people. And . . . and . . . I guess I'll miss you guys."

"You will?" I said in shock.

Mary Anne dug her elbow into my side and I closed my big mouth. Fortunately, Sean didn't seem to notice.

"Yeah. I mean, even if you are baby-sitters, you're not so bad. I had fun. And you weren't mean to me about, you know, things that I did that weren't so good. And I liked being King of the Hour."

"Oh, Sean," said the softhearted Mary Anne. (Okay, I admit it. I was touched as well.) "We're going to miss you too."

"You will?" asked Sean, sounding just as surprised as I had.

"Of course we will," said Mary Anne. "There's nobody like you. You may not have been the easiest kid we didn't baby-sit for, but things were always interesting when you were around."

Well, *that* was true.

"Sean," I said, "when I moved to Stoneybrook, I *hated* leaving my home and all my friends. I pitched about seven different fits trying to convince my mother not to take her new job. It didn't work. We moved just the same. And you know what? I'm glad we did."

Now both Mary Anne and Sean gave me surprised looks. Mary Anne said, "You are?"

"Sure," I answered. "I miss my old friends. But I've made some terrific new friends. And I've had a lot of fun doing it."

Sean didn't look quite so glum. "Maybe I'll make new friends," he mumbled.

"Maybe you will," I said. "You won't know until you check it out, will you?"

He smiled a little. "I guess not."

"How's your appetite now?" I asked.

"Better," Sean replied, his smile growing.

"Good," I said. "Have a cookie."

At that moment, Lou ran by. She grabbed a handful of cookies and streaked away shouting "Cookie Monster, Cookie Monster, Cookie Monster!" Karen and Hannie took up the chant.

"Hey!" Sean said, and took off after them.

I looked at Mary Anne and we smiled.

"Hey," said Mary Anne. "I'm glad too."

I went jogging the next morning, still spinning on the energy of accomplishment — my video project (an A, with high praise, from Dolly One), a successful going-away party for Sean and Corrie, and the decision to take it a little easier. I turned up one familiar road and down another, checking out who had brought their newspapers inside, who was sleeping late, waving to dogs I knew, avoiding familiar bumps and ruts in the sidewalk.

A moving van drove by. Was it the Nichollses, moving in? Or some other family new to Stoneybrook?

I waved and the driver honked. Then I dodged around a mailbox and kept running. Whoever it was, they'd picked a good place to live. My kind of town.

Come to think of it, it *was* my town. I wasn't the new kid anymore.

I belonged.

I picked up my pace and ran home.

Dear Reader,

Abby and the Best Kid Ever is the second book in which Lou McNally appears. She was first introduced in #62 *Kristy and the Worst Kid Ever.* So many readers asked for another book about Lou that I finally wrote one. My editors and I are always surprised to see which new character strikes a chord with readers. Another character who, like Lou, appealed to kids was Danielle Roberts, who appeared first in #48 *Jessi's Wish* and then, after lots of requests from readers, in #82 *Jessi and the Troublemaker.* Another character who has appealed to readers is Susan Felder from #32 *Kristy and the Secret of Susan.* So far, Susan hasn't had another book of her own, but she will make an appearance in Super Special #15, *Baby-sitters' European Vacation!*

There are some other newer characters my editors and I like a lot. So far they have appeared once, but we hope someday to bring them back. One of them is Amy Porter, Dawn's cousin, from #87 *Stacey and the Bad Girls.* Mara, Kyle, and Brenda from *Stacey and the Mystery at the Mall* might also show up again. Unfortunately, we probably won't see Corrie and Sean Addison again, since they are moving out of Stoneybrook. Sometimes it's sad to see characters go, but it's great to meet new ones.

Happy reading,

Ann M. Martin

L. GODWIN

Ann M. Martin

About the Author

ANN MATTHEWS MARTIN was born on August 12, 1955. She grew up in Princeton, NJ, with her parents and her younger sister, Jane.

Although Ann used to be a teacher and then an editor of children's books, she's now a full-time writer. She gets the ideas for her books from many different places. Some are based on personal experiences. Others are based on childhood memories and feelings. Many are written about contemporary problems or events.

All of Ann's characters, even the members of the Baby-sitters Club, are made up. (So is Stoneybrook.) But many of her characters are based on real people. Sometimes Ann names her characters after people she knows, other times she chooses names she likes.

In addition to the Baby-sitters Club books, Ann Martin has written many other books for children. Her favorite is *Ten Kids, No Pets* because she loves big families and she loves animals. Her favorite Baby-sitters Club book is *Kristy's Big Day*. (By the way, Kristy is her favorite baby-sitter!)

Ann M. Martin now lives in New York with her cats, Gussie and Woody. Her hobbies are reading, sewing, and needlework — especially making clothes for children.

Notebook Pages

This Baby-sitters Club book belongs to _____.

I am _____ years old and in the _____

grade.

The name of my school is _____.

I got this BSC book from _____.

I started reading it on _____ and

finished reading it on _____.

The place where I read most of this book is _____.

My favorite part was when _____.

If I could change anything in the story, it might be the part when

_____.

My favorite character in the Baby-sitters Club is _____.

The BSC member I am most like is _____

because _____.

If I could write a Baby-sitters Club book it would be about _____

_____.

#116 Abby and the Best Kid Ever

Abby is surprised when she finds that Lou McNally, who was once the Worst Kid Ever, is now the Best Kid Ever. Still, she is happy that Lou has moved back to Stoneybrook. This is how I feel about Lou: _____

_____. The members of the BSC are also sad that Corrie and Sean Addison are moving away. One person I wish would move out of Stoneybrook is _____

_____. If I had a chance to move away from my town, I would move to _____ because

_____. If I could choose anyone new to move to Stoneybrook, I would choose _____

_____ because _____

_____

_____.

ABBY'S

Twins from the start!

My dad could always make me laugh.

SCRAPBOOK

Tennis, anyone?

My dad's favorite place.

Look out Hawaii! Here comes the BSC.

Illustrations by Angelo Tilley

Read all the books
about **Abby**
in the Baby-sitters Club series
by Ann M. Martin

Look for #117

CLAUDIA AND THE TERRIBLE TRUTH

"I'm going to ask one more time," said Mr. Nichols. And then he began to shout, "WHO LEFT THE —"

"I did," I said quickly. "It was me. I'm sorry. I was making us a snack when the doorbell rang, and —"

"No problem," said Mr. Nicholls in a totally normal voice. His anger seemed to have disappeared instantly. "Please forgive me for hollering," he said with a little grin. "I thought it was one of my dumb, slobby sons who did it."

That shocked me. I'd never heard a parent talk that way before. But Nate and Joey didn't even seem to notice.

"Now, can I offer you a ride home?" asked Mr. Nicholls. Now he sounded relaxed, even friendly.

"Thanks, no," I said quickly. "I can walk. It's not far." That screaming act had scared me a little, to be perfectly honest. I wasn't too thrilled at the idea of being alone in a car with Mr. Nicholls right then.

On my way out, I remembered something. "Hey," I said to the boys and their father. "Tomorrow there's going to be a planning meeting for the Saint Patrick's Day parade. I'll take you boys, if you'd like to come — and if that's okay," I added quickly, looking over at Mr. Nicholls. "They'll meet lots of kids there," I pointed out.

"I suppose it's all right," said Mr. Nicholls. I could tell he was still trying to be nice. "As long as you promise to tell me if my boys misbehave."

"Sure," I said. I knew Joey and Nate would behave just fine. They were good kids. I glanced at them on my way out, and when I saw their faces I could tell they were sorry to see me leave. I knew then that it wasn't some bad experience with a baby-sitter that was making them so nervous.

It wasn't me they were afraid of.

Collect them all!

❑ MG43388-1	#1	Kristy's Great Idea	$3.50
❑ MG43387-3	#10	Logan Likes Mary Anne!	$3.99
❑ MG43717-8	#15	Little Miss Stoneybrook...and Dawn	$3.50
❑ MG43722-4	#20	Kristy and the Walking Disaster	$3.50
❑ MG43347-4	#25	Mary Anne and the Search for Tigger	$3.50
❑ MG42498-X	#30	Mary Anne and the Great Romance	$3.50
❑ MG42508-0	#35	Stacey and the Mystery of Stoneybrook	$3.50
❑ MG44082-9	#40	Claudia and the Middle School Mystery	$3.25
❑ MG43574-4	#45	Kristy and the Baby Parade	$3.50
❑ MG44969-9	#50	Dawn's Big Date	$3.50
❑ MG44968-0	#51	Stacey's Ex-Best Friend	$3.50
❑ MG44966-4	#52	Mary Anne + 2 Many Babies	$3.50
❑ MG44967-2	#53	Kristy for President	$3.25
❑ MG44965-6	#54	Mallory and the Dream Horse	$3.25
❑ MG44964-8	#55	Jessi's Gold Medal	$3.25
❑ MG45657-1	#56	Keep Out, Claudia!	$3.50
❑ MG45658-X	#57	Dawn Saves the Planet	$3.50
❑ MG45659-8	#58	Stacey's Choice	$3.50
❑ MG45660-1	#59	Mallory Hates Boys (and Gym)	$3.50
❑ MG45662-8	#60	Mary Anne's Makeover	$3.50
❑ MG45663-6	#61	Jessi and the Awful Secret	$3.50
❑ MG45664-4	#62	Kristy and the Worst Kid Ever	$3.50
❑ MG45665-2	#63	Claudia's Freind Friend	$3.50
❑ MG45666-0	#64	Dawn's Family Feud	$3.50
❑ MG45667-9	#65	Stacey's Big Crush	$3.50
❑ MG47004-3	#66	Maid Mary Anne	$3.50
❑ MG47005-1	#67	Dawn's Big Move	$3.50
❑ MG47006-X	#68	Jessi and the Bad Baby-sitter	$3.50
❑ MG47007-8	#69	Get Well Soon, Mallory!	$3.50
❑ MG47008-6	#70	Stacey and the Cheerleaders	$3.50
❑ MG47009-4	#71	Claudia and the Perfect Boy	$3.99
❑ MG47010-8	#72	Dawn and the We ❤ Kids Club	$3.99
❑ MG47011-6	#73	Mary Anne and Miss Priss	$3.99
❑ MG47012-4	#74	Kristy and the Copycat	$3.99
❑ MG47013-2	#75	Jessi's Horrible Prank	$3.50
❑ MG47014-0	#76	Stacey's Lie	$3.50
❑ MG48221-1	#77	Dawn and Whitney, Friends Forever	$3.99
❑ MG48222-X	#78	Claudia and Crazy Peaches	$3.50
❑ MG48223-8	#79	Mary Anne Breaks the Rules	$3.50
❑ MG48224-6	#80	Mallory Pike, #1 Fan	$3.99
❑ MG48225-4	#81	Kristy and Mr. Mom	$3.50
❑ MG48226-2	#82	Jessi and the Troublemaker	$3.99
❑ MG48235-1	#83	Stacey vs. the BSC	$3.50
❑ MG48228-9	#84	Dawn and the School Spirit War	$3.50
❑ MG48236-X	#85	Claudi Kishi, Live from WSTO	$3.50
❑ MG48227-0	#86	Mary Anne and Camp BSC	$3.50
❑ MG48237-8	#87	Stacey and the Bad Girls	$3.50
❑ MG22872-2	#88	Farewell, Dawn	$3.50

More titles... ▶

The Baby-sitters Club titles continued...

❏ MG22873-0	#89	Kristy and the Dirty Diapers	$3.50
❏ MG22874-9	#90	Welcome to the BSC, Abby	$3.99
❏ MG22875-1	#91	Claudia and the First Thanksgiving	$3.50
❏ MG22876-5	#92	Mallory's Christmas Wish	$3.50
❏ MG22877-3	#93	Mary Anne and the Memory Garden	$3.99
❏ MG22878-1	#94	Stacey McGill, Super Sitter	$3.99
❏ MG22879-X	#95	Kristy + Bart = ?	$3.99
❏ MG22880-3	#96	Abby's Lucky Thirteen	$3.99
❏ MG22881-1	#97	Claudia and the World's Cutest Baby	$3.99
❏ MG22882-X	#98	Dawn and Too Many Sitters	$3.99
❏ MG69205-4	#99	Stacey's Broken Heart	$3.99
❏ MG69206-2	#100	Kristy's Worst Idea	$3.99
❏ MG69207-0	#101	Claudia Kishi, Middle School Dropout	$3.99
❏ MG69208-9	#102	Mary Anne and the Little Princess	$3.99
❏ MG69209-7	#103	Happy Holidays, Jessi	$3.99
❏ MG69210-0	#104	Abby's Twin	$3.99
❏ MG69211-9	#105	Stacey the Math Whiz	$3.99
❏ MG69212-7	#106	Claudia, Queen of the Seventh Grade	$3.99
❏ MG69213-5	#107	Mind Your Own Business, Kristy!	$3.99
❏ MG69214-3	#108	Don't Give Up, Mallory	$3.99
❏ MG69215-1	#109	Mary Anne to the Rescue	$3.99
❏ MG05988-2	#110	Abby the Bad Sport	$3.99
❏ MG05989-0	#111	Stacey's Secret Friend	$3.99
❏ MG05990-4	#112	Kristy and the Sister War	$3.99
❏ MG45575-3		Logan's Story Special Edition Readers' Request	$3.25
❏ MG47118-X		Logan Bruno, Boy Baby-sitter Special Edition Readers' Request	$3.50
❏ MG47756-0		Shannon's Story Special Edition	$3.50
❏ MG47686-6		The Baby-sitters Club Guide to Baby-sitting	$3.25
❏ MG47314-X		The Baby-sitters Club Trivia and Puzzle Fun Book	$2.50
❏ MG48400-1		BSC Portrait Collection: Claudia's Book	$3.50
❏ MG22864-1		BSC Portrait Collection: Dawn's Book	$3.50
❏ MG69181-3		BSC Portrait Collection: Kristy's Book	$3.99
❏ MG22865-X		BSC Portrait Collection: Mary Anne's Book	$3.99
❏ MG48399-4		BSC Portrait Collection: Stacey's Book	$3.50
❏ MG69182-1		BSC Portrait Collection: Abby's Book	$3.99
❏ MG92713-2		The Complete Guide to The Baby-sitters Club	$4.95
❏ MG47151-1		The Baby-sitters Club Chain Letter	$14.95
❏ MG48295-5		The Baby-sitters Club Secret Santa	$14.95
❏ MG45074-3		The Baby-sitters Club Notebook	$2.50
❏ MG44783-1		The Baby-sitters Club Postcard Book	$4.95

Available wherever you buy books...or use this order form.
Scholastic Inc., P.O. Box 7502, Jefferson City, MO 65102

Please send me the books I have checked above. I am enclosing $_____
(please add $2.00 to cover shipping and handling). Send check or money order–
no cash or C.O.D.s please.

Name_____ Birthdate_____

Address_____

City_____ State/Zip_____

Please allow four to six weeks for delivery. Offer good in the U.S. only. Sorry,
mail orders are not available to residents of Canada. Prices subject to change.

BSC5962

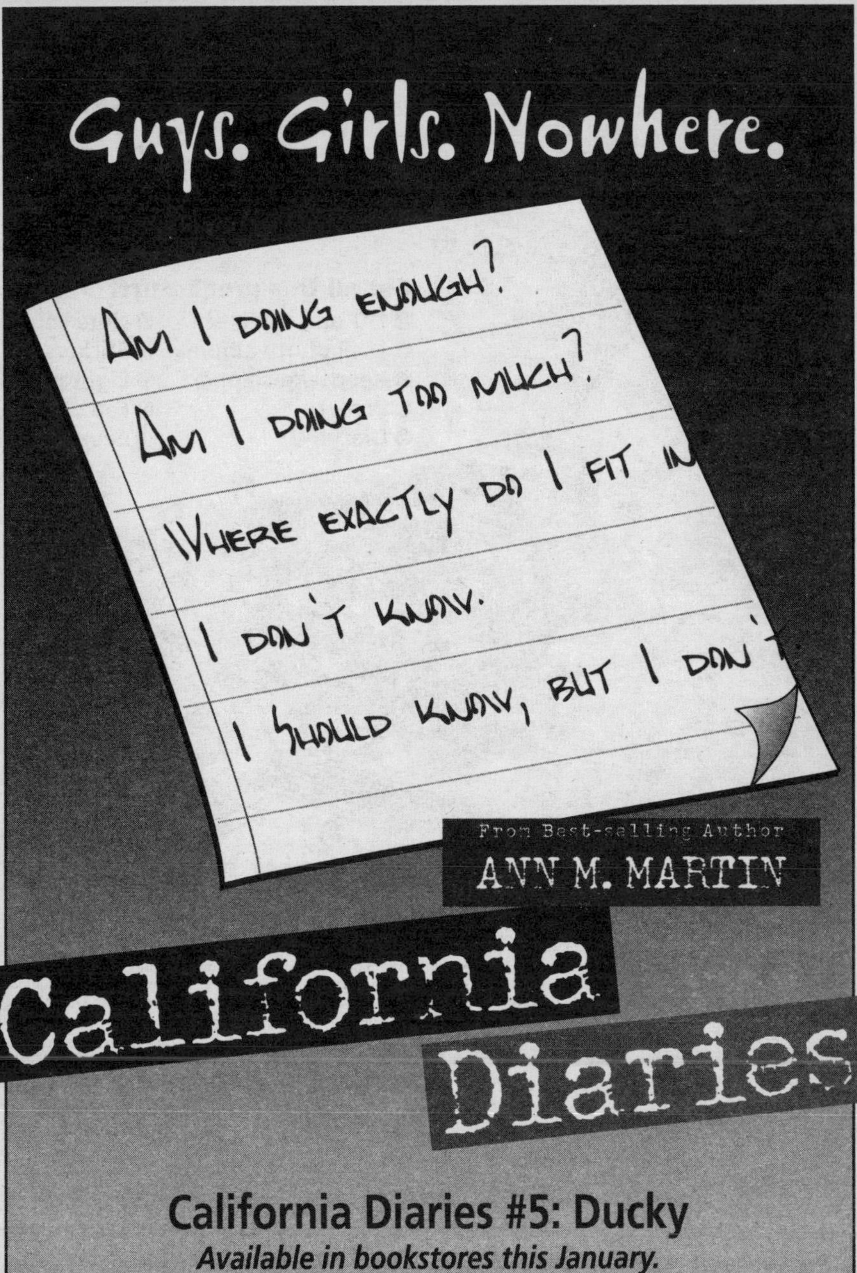

CD5697
SCHOLASTIC

JOIN THE FAN CLUB! SIGN UP NOW!

THE BABY-SITTERS CLUB®
FAN CLUB

Only $8.95!
Plus $2.00 Postage and Handling

Get all this great stuff!
❶ 110-mm camera!
❷ Mini photo album!
❸ Keepsake shipper!
❹ Poster!
❺ Diary!
❻ Note cards!
❼ Stickers!
❽ Eight pencil
❾ Fan Club newsletter!

Exclusive news and trivia! Exclusive contests! Interviews with Ann Martin! Letters from fans!

To get your fan club pack (in the U.S. and Canada only), just fill out the coupon or write the information on a 3" x 5" card and send it to us with your check or money order. U.S. residents: $8.95 plus $2.00 postage and handling to The New BSC FAN CLUB, Scholastic Inc. P.O Box 7500, Jefferson City, MO 65102. Canadian residents: $13.95 plus $2.00 postage and handling to The New BSC FAN CLUB, Scholastic Canada, 123 Newkirk Road, Richmond Hill, Ontario, L4C3G5. Offer expires 9/30/97. Offer good for one year from date of receipt. Please allow 4-6 weeks for your introductory pack to arrive.

* First newsletter is sent after introductory pack. You will receive at least 4 newsletters during your one-year membership.

Hurry! Send me my Baby-Sitter's Fan Club Pack. I am enclosing my check or money order (no cash please) for U.S. residents: $10.95 ($8.95 plus $2.00) and for Canadian residents: $15.95 ($13.95 plus $2.00).

Name_____ Birthdate_____
           First   Last   D/M/Y

Address_____

City_____ State_____ Zip_____

Telephone (   )_____ Boy_____ Girl_____

Where did you buy this book? ❑ Bookstore ❑ Book Fair ❑ Book Club ❑ Other_____

SCHOLASTIC
B11629